Nathanial Thatcher 4

The Fourth Rebellion

T. C. Chappell

Blue DOT Books

Nathanial Thatcher 4

The Fourth Rebellion

"The greatest danger to our future is apathy."

-Jane Goodall

CONTENTS

Nathanial Thatcher 4

The Fourth Rebellion

T. C. Chappell

SANCTUARY

Nathanial Thatcher ran as if the fate of the world depended on it. A silver and gold staff was tucked tight against his right arm, deep etchings of men in battle spiraling up its length. Suede belts woven with chainmail crisscrossed around his legs, arms, and chest, providing light but protective armor.

Nathanial saw attackers flanking him from both sides, coordinated and closing in on him. A staff swung toward his knees; he jumped, kicked off a passing tree trunk, and landed on an inclining rock. He ran to its apex and leaped toward the hanging brush, which he quickly mowed through by rapidly twisting his own staff.

Hitting the ground, Nathanial didn't miss a beat. More dark figures approached from every angle. It was an ambush! He had to get up and out of there.

Using his staff as a pole vault, he flung himself up onto a mushroom. The canopy of the fungi tilted groundward from his sudden weight upon it; he used its righting momentum to aid his jump high into an adjacent tree. Nathanial darted down the branch in front of him and spotted a clearing just a few trees ahead. He kept to the branches, jumping from one to the next to the next. The mounting pressure was pushing him on. He still had company amongst the canopy. He needed a drastic move to lose them.

With the final branch coming to an end like a ship's plank, Nathanial readied himself for the dive. His staff shrank down into a smooth gold and silver hilted knife that he quickly stowed into the sheath strapped to his chest. Then, he took the leap.

It was like an Olympic high diver jumping with confidence, knowing there was a pool below him, only there was no luxury of water for Nathanial. His surety came from a bronze and silver teardrop shield upon his back. It seemed like one solid object at first, but quickly opened up into the veins of his dragonfly-like wings, the shining metal thickly outlining their shape all the way around and down into their pointed tips.

Gliding downward, wings spread firm, Nathanial leaned into gravity's pull. He accelerated to the point that his deep brown eyes began to sting, tears pooling in the corners where a golden skin tone was just noticeable beyond his fair yet sun-kissed complexion.

His heart rate pounded now: he was pushing his limits. The ground rushed toward him and, just as the green of the grass encompassed all of his vision, Nathanial fiercely pushed his wings into rapid action and arched his body upward to fly just a breath above the grass line. He knew there was only one pursuer left out of the entire lot who'd chased him that could continue the hunt now, but that one held the weight of all the rest of them combined.

Nathanial could almost feel outstretched fingers grasping at his ankles, but he dared not look back. Safety was just ahead, where the grass was cut down to the ground and a red painted circle beckoned. That's where he needed to make it to, and he was almost there.

Nathanial was coming in too fast, but he couldn't risk slowing… this was going to be a rough landing. He was past the tall grass and dipped down. Nathanial hit the center of the red circle and forcibly dug his fingers into the earth to stop himself from rolling out. Panting like a horse at the finish line, he got to his knees, smiling, and watched his competition land gracefully in front of him.

"Ha! I did it," Nathanial said.

The tall blue sprite before him pushed his thick hair back from a skeptical face. His leather armor was stained a deep navy, and a cutlass hung taut to his hip. Nathanial pushed to his feet, pulled a blue flag out from an armored fold in his chest, and threw it at the sprite's booted feet.

"I got your artifact." Nathanial's smile broadened across his bold face. "Admit it, Boss. I beat you."

Boss licked his lips and looked behind him. The rest of the competing sprites trickled out of the tall grass, grand enough to be called a forest for how high it towered over the inch-tall sprites.

"Great job," Aliya panted, her Hebrew accent thicker from exhaustion. She came to rest by the circle alongside the group, her brown hair braided with silver ribbons. Her armor was much the same as Nathanial's, and she had a bow crossed over her chest. "You finally did it! Mila was sure you'd need Sidian to beat Boss."

Mila looked rebellious as ever on approach. No weapons or armor dared replace her black cut-up vest or her hole-ridden pants that she tucked into her high purple boots. It was a wonder she kept up with the pack at all. The weight of her clumping necklaces looked heavy, but also nicely set off her purple skin, an attribute which spread further around her eyes, ears, and fingernails than they had just months before.

"I almost had you," Mila said, pointing at Nathanial. "Lucky jump."

A bronze Bunny and golden Gem arrived, both clad in wooden plates of armor. Bunny's fluffy hair, brown and sparkling, bounced as she put up her hand for Nathanial. "Give me some up top, Nate-a-roonie! Awesome dive!"

Nathanial clapped his hand against hers and beamed excitedly. "Where's Spassel and Phlegm?" he asked, looking through the dozen faces that made up his convening opponents.

"Spassel got caught in a trap," Gem explained in her delicate voice. Her shimmering hair was twisted up in ropes, and her wings were just noticeable upon her back. Nathanial had recently learned that Gem's wings were almost as new to her as his own were to him, but she didn't like to use them. They'd sprouted soon after she changed her blood ability from crystal sprite to wish sprite, and she didn't make them a priority when learning her new abilities. "Mr. Phlegm is trying to cut him down now."

"Oh." Nathanial laughed. "I wondered what

that yelp was. Anyway, Boss still can't admit I won. Bunny, tell him!"

Bunny chuckled and looked to Boss, who was pulling off a pair of blue gloves. He pointed subtly down at Nathanial's ankle. Bunny followed his finger and put her hands to her mouth, saying, "Oooohhhh, Natey-boy!"

"What?" Nathanial asked, looking down. A blue handprint circled his ankle. "No! No way! That had to have happened after I was already in the circle. That doesn't count!"

Boss shrugged. "You were still in the air. You're down a foot."

"Not fair," Nathanial protested.

"Add that to your other missing extremities from the past ten games and I'd say you've got, what… a floating head left?" Boss grinned.

"I had you beat! I got your artifact. I won this one! Boss, come on," Nathanial whined.

Boss laughed and tussled Nathanial's curly dirty-blonde head, causing some of the sweaty orange highlights from his recent growth to stand up like flames. "Oh, don't be so hard-headed. Admit the loss. That way when you really win it will actually mean something. You're getting better all the time."

Nathanial pulled his headband off and threw

it to the ground as Boss took flight.

Aliya stepped closer. "You know he just gives you a hard time to make you stronger," she said kindly, and pushed back the tuft of rogue blue in his hair that stuck out by his temple.

"He gives me a hard time because he enjoys it," Nathanial countered.

"But he's right," Aliya added. "You *are* getting better all the time. You did great. One mark right at the end is amazing. The game pits everyone against each other, and when you got your hands on the artifact it became everyone against you. Yet you made it to the finish with the goal in hand. You should be proud."

"One mark could be the end, Aliya. All it took was one touch for Seizette to lock Spassel into a block of diamond. I have to do better."

Mila closed in and put an elbow on Nathanial's shoulder. "Is he still whining?" She goaded him with a smirk.

Nathanial moved so that her elbow fell. "I don't ever see you getting through mark free, Mila."

"Yeah, and I don't expect to," Mila chortled. "Boss has decades of experience on us, Nat. I'd worry if we could beat him after just a few months of training."

"She has a point there," Aliya agreed.

Bunny interrupted the debate with a clap. "Let's go get some grub, bubs!"

They walked together underneath the swirling gold and purple of a sunset sky and down the center of a long field on their way toward the largest mound of their newly founded village of Sanctuary, duly called Sanctuary Hill. Their kitchens, dining hall, dorms for the youth, and classes were sheltered there, along with secret meeting spaces and the hall of delegates.

The field was surrounded by little grassy bumps that were, in fact, apartments for the many volunteers who had come to help the displaced sprites. These hideaways always called back memories of Hobbiton for Nathanial, a town full of small folk from one of his favorite book series, but here the scale down was even greater than that of The Shire, giving Sanctuary an even more unique beauty. Giant flowers grew out of the roofs, concealing from above the doors and windows within the grassy huts that would have given them away as something more than natural formations. This tendency to use floral camouflage caused charming moments throughout the day, when pollen would flurry down like golden snowfall.

Mealtimes tended to be an exciting part of living in this underground Sanctuary. The eating space grew almost daily to make room for the slow influx of refugees who were escaping Lady Seizette's ever-tightening grip on sprite society. The architects of the dining room were collaborating caver sprites and digger sprites. The diggers sent their moles to carve out the amoeba-shaped space while the cavers chewed up and spat out the rock to form bumpy column-like support beams and squat stalagmites for tables and chairs. Nathanial was often fascinated by the tiny sparkling crystals that coated most of the rocky formations. That, combined with the inner glow from the walls, made him feel like they were all eating in a magically warmed igloo.

It wasn't just the unique design of the room that interested Nathanial; it was mostly the topics of conversation that flared up over the multiple course meals. Nathanial and his close friends Aliya, Mila, and Spassel were in the minority at Sanctuary: they were teenaged sprites in a cavernous room filled mostly with adults who seemed to forget that there were youths around as their tankards were refilled multiple times throughout a meal.

Nathanial took advantage of this happy overlook by sitting at a table in an alcove that was within peeking distance of the Head Councilor's table, where all the important sprites sat. The scoop of the wall had the added benefit of bouncing acoustics from said table directly into eager eavesdropping ears.

The first course of fried arachnid with artichoke dip had gone off with the usual pleasantries, but Nathanial had noticed a new delegate at the Head Councilor's table; he'd announced a gift of his favorite mead and kept insisting on refills after every drained cup. It was only a matter of time before the talk would turn to business.

Nathanial brought his head back from around the spying corner and let his attention return to Spassel's long-winded tale of that afternoon's mishap. The little sprite spoke in quick, run-on sentences that always made Nathanial think he'd turn red from lack of breath, but no such coloration ever marred the almost albino complexion of the enthusiastic storyteller. "And then I thought for sure he'd go up into the canopy, and so he did, but before that, I knew I'd set the fifth trap too low and he was about to jump right over it, so I thought if I could use the fourth trap to fling myself forward and head him off, I could reset the fifth trap in time to snag him, but the mechanism in the fourth trap had been kicked loose at some point and — oh, look, coconut-rolled honeysuckle pistols, those are my favorite!"

A basket of what looked like a dozen coconut macaroons replaced the crumb-scattered tray that had, minutes before, been a battered king crab-sized arachnid.

"Thanks, Pat," Aliya said to the grass-pigmented volunteer server. "Great job out on the field today."

"Thanks, Aliya. You're getting great with that bow!"

"If you hadn't given me that pointer about my elbow, I'd still be shooting the *whiskers off the rat*, as you like to put it."

They laughed, and the volunteer left.

"*Anyway.*" Spassel attempted to pick up where he'd left off, but with the addition of a bulging cheek.

"Hold up, Spassel," Nathanial said, putting a hand up. He put his ear close to the corner again. "I think they're finally getting to the good stuff." Nathanial craned his head around the wall of his alcove and watched eagerly. The newest sprite at the Head Councilors' table had garnered the attention of his peers.

"Most of you here know me, but for those I am unacquainted with, allow me to introduce myself: I am Larix, Delegate from Ashwald," he said, and raised his cup in greeting.

Nathanial had no idea where Ashwald was, and he couldn't place the accent, but the sprite had an ancient air about him.

Larix towered over most of the other sprites at his table, even as he sat. His skin had patches of tree bark protruding in places like his cheekbones and collarbones. Much about him felt like the ancient woods, with gray tones in dreadlocks that looked more like oak sticks that grew long and twisted from his head. Even his floor-skimming trench coat grew lichen, as if it believed the sprite to be a tree.

"We find ourselves in a time of great strife. How did we get to this point? When I consider our roots, back to that pond where our ancestors grew contentedly and the sun fed us life, the world was slow and simple and uneventful. That was peace. But then one of us picked up their stem, split it in two, and took a stroll to explore the pond next door. Curiosity drove us and took us wide across the lands and sea, branching us off into different classes.

"Then we found something beyond peace: Our

blood abilities gave us purpose, to aid the new life springing up all around us—the elves, the goblins, the humans—all of whom searched to define themselves as we had. We were at our best in those times."

Larix took a pause and gazed at his fellow sprites. "The first rebellion, when the humans split from faery to grow into the larger world around us, shook our foundation. But we adapted. Many of us developed anew, keen to negotiate with the humans."

Mila rolled her eyes and said, "What is this guy, some sort of history teacher?"

"He's setting the stage," Spassel whispered. "Reminding everyone what we've been through."

"Shh." Nathanial waved a hand at them.

"Humans' gift for storytelling enchanted many sprites," Larix continued. "Some wanted to be the heroes in their tales. They became attached to a single human life, and would work to make him or her prosperous in exchange for a home in which to raise their own family, a home with the human. The fire sprites and love sprites would often battle over one human's affection. And so humans began to see their hold over sprites, and took advantage. They would take a love sprite pact, enjoy the match that was made for them, then banish the sprite from the home they had helped to build, regarded as a pest rather than a partner. *That's* when the cracks began to form."

"Well," Aliya thought aloud, "who wants little people spying on them all the time? It's creepy."

"It's no different than living with other humans," Mila said. "The sprites were supposed to have their own space within the house. And we still do, only humans don't get to know about it anymore."

Here the Head Councilor cleared his throat. That small sound commanded everyone's attention. He wore an antlered crown low to his brow, and his black pepper hair feathered back around the temples of his sharp hazel eyes. He had a calm, commanding posture that echoed the deliberate words of his voice. "Greed and selfish behavior were not only baring their teeth from the humans. We saw the same ugliness from all walks of faery. That competition to be the dominant species is what shook our world into a second rebellion and put a monarchy into power. Promises to put sprites first, above all others, may have raised us out of that ugly mess, but it also sparked another flame that has been very hard to put out since: spite. The Queen wanted the world for herself, and to do that she needed to turn all sprites against her remaining competition: the humans. The monarchy labeled the humans as factories, and thus the dehumanizing process began."

Larix nodded. "Yes, that is true," he agreed, "and perhaps even then we knew it was wrong to dehumanize them, even if there was bad blood between us. But we were in recovery. We had lost our purpose and our peace. It took decades to find normalcy again and, in that time, humans became nothing more than a job to us; a way to make ends meet. The Third Rebellion didn't happen because we saw treating the humans like factories as wrong, it happened because the monarchy abused this power beyond what the working class thought lawful, to the result of an unfair advantage."

Boss interjected. "Are you saying we should continue to ignore the blatant human abuse that was established by the monarchy?"

"I'm saying that what the monarchy did to the humans shouldn't even be the core issue of our current strife. The monarchy is supposed to be demolished, but it seems the Crossing Treaty was a mere chess piece in a larger game. I'm saying that Seizette stirs rumors of a Fourth Rebellion, not because a rebellion is imminent but because she wants unrest. What better method to put herself back in the game? She rose to power out of chaos once. Why not again?"

The Head Councilor knitted his fingers together and said, "We wouldn't even have to worry about her rumors if the power of governance was truly still in the public's hands. Seizette's supporters have made it into the elected chairs of our council, and the balance of our system is leaning in her favor. We are a stone's throw away from the council being nothing more than a puppet whose strings are pulled by a tyrant."

Surprisingly, Phlegm piped up. His Brooklyn accent and greasy green features seemed particularly unrefined in his present company. "Well, whose fault is that? I say we got too comfortable. Stopped paying attention to our governing, turned a blind eye to it all. Those council seats were up for grabs and the powerful took 'em. No one's fault but our own."

Boss took a large breath and said, "Now, Phlegm, I don't think the public are completely to blame here. There were manipulations at work that no one saw coming. But I promise you, Seizette does not control our government yet." Boss turned his attention back to the group at large. "That is why this coming election is so important. We must have solidarity when it's time to convene at Mount Lassen. All of these matters will be addressed at the council meeting after dinner."

"Will you be there?" Larix asked.

"I'm not a delegate or a council member," Boss explained.

"Which is why I put these thoughts out now," Larix said. "So often those left unheard are the ones that should be doing the talking."

"He'll be there," said the Head Councilor.

Boss acknowledged the Head Councilor with a bow of his head.

"Good." Larix went back to his drink and the general chatter began again.

Nathanial let out a long sigh and turned back to his friends. "I don't know. Is it really just rumors, like they say? There are a lot of people here at Sanctuary for there not to be a rebellion brewing. I mean, if there isn't, there should be."

"I know, right?" Spassel said after a quick gulp of juice. "Seizette says we're a bunch of troublemakers that want to take away livelihoods by making pro-factory products, like they require less of a workforce, and saying we want to change our blood traits so we can steal the best jobs out from under those born into the positions, but anyone who knows how to read a data chart can see pro-factory products create more jobs because you need rotating sources, and if everyone works a job they want rather than one they're forced into, then you get a happy workforce, and a happy workforce is more productive. It's all just ridiculous! Look at the facts, people, don't listen to hearsay."

"Right." Nathanial nodded. Even if he hadn't quite caught all of it, he got the gist.

Pat appeared and put down a large tray of assorted cheeses, bread, minced bug bits, and central dipping sauces that smelled of garlic.

"What's wrong, Nathan?" Pat asked.

"Don't worry about him," Mila said, taking one of the dipping bowls for herself. "He's just got one of those spider claws from earlier stuck up his rump."

Nathanial coughed out the fizzy drink he'd been sipping as Mila giggled. Pat shook her head and moved on.

"Mila!" Nathanial wiped his mouth. "Why are you being so mean?"

Mila calmed her laugh and swallowed. She read Nathanial's hurt expression, then said, "I'm sorry, okay? You're just being so, so… self-important. It's getting on my nerves. But I'll ease off."

"Self-important?" Nathanial exclaimed.

"Yeah. You think you have to be better than everyone in the games, and you're always trying to listen in on the adults like it's your business."

Nathanial gaped and his cheeks turned red.

"Hey, everyone should be trying their best on the field. And guess what? They aren't games! It's training against a real threat. I let you look in my head so you could see what they're doing at Swartza High. How can you not be concerned after that? I tried to explain it to Boss, too, but he just assured me the council has it under control. He's always downplaying things, just like he did right now to the delegates over there."

Mila bit her pinky nail. "Look, you know I'm the first to jump in when there's a fight that needs fighting. But I agree with Boss on this one. See, from where I'm sitting"—she pointed toward the Head Councilors table—"I can see some real deal sprite leaders who have seen the worst-case scenario and made peace in a time when people thought we'd meet our end. I'm pretty sure they're going to nip this thing in the bud, especially since they have the most nectar Skilla who has ever walked the face of the planet with them!"

Nathanial glanced over to the mature purple sprite, Amaranth, who Mila had been elated to see arrive just days before. She was beautiful in an intimidating and deadly sort of way; tiny spines coated the deep purple cactus petals flanking her shoulders and sporadically adorned braids of her long raven black hair. Her dress draped heavily, and was woven with a variety of elements, from leather to alkaline metals.

It was strange to see what Mila could expect for a skin color pallet. She already possessed the dark purple shading around her eyes, forehead, and fingernails, but she didn't yet have the smooth violet cheeks or high lilac lashes.

"Amaranth was right in the thick of it at the height of the Third Rebellion." Mila spoke from the edge of her seat. "She heard all of Seizette's plans firsthand, including the decree that would have put sprites in jail just for speaking out against the monarchy! So you know I would join any rebellion against the Swartza if I thought it was necessary. I'm the one who tried to tell you how slimy the Swartza are, remember? Right before you ran off to meet them anyway?"

Nathanial clicked his tongue. She had a good point. It wasn't long ago that Nathanial was the one who'd refused to get involved while Mila had tried to convince him otherwise. But so much had happened to him since her speech on the train. She had told him then that he wouldn't want to run home once he knew the truth about how bad the Swartza were, and she was right. So why wouldn't she fight with him now? Were Amaranth and the others really so impressive that she no longer worried about the threat of Seizette?

"Well I'm not saying they aren't capable, only I think it wouldn't hurt if we tried to help. It sounds like most sprites are clueless about what's going on in the government right now. How will they know how to vote if they don't know the truth?"

"If I may interject," Spassel said, swallowing and straightening his disheveled bangs. "I see both points here, so first let's acknowledge the issues. Seizette has succeeded in spreading the idea that it's okay to abuse factories, making it appear to be the only way that sprites can be successful, even to the extent of lying about factory-friendly places shutting down from lack of profits when actually it was an elaborate smear campaign led by headquarters to create the new Grit-the-Gook-Whoa monopoly. Since those who are keenly aware of these facts are in hiding, that leaves the vast majority of the general public left in oblivion."

"Yeah, we know. What are you trying to get at, Spaz?" Mila snatched the last piece of bread from Spassel's plate.

Spassel put up a finger and continued. "Nathanial claims that we—as in us at this table, though we may seem like four insignificant teenagers—should be a part of the fight against Seizette because there are so tragically few of us in the know out there.

"Mila, for the opposing point, is saying that we four are not needed because the brightest minds who led our former battles sit just feet away from us, and therefore we can expect the situation to be resolved without our aid.

"Since there has been a call of no confidence in our current Head Councilor and the vote for a new one will be in two weeks' time, I propose a debate. Evidence must be presented by each of you, for and against our involvement, to be held at the end of this week. That will give us another week to take action before a new Head Councilor is voted in, if necessary."

"What?" both Nathanial and Mila asked uncertainly.

"Just hear me out," Spassel said, beaming. "Nathanial must present evidence that the council is unable to properly inform the public of what is transpiring within our government and that Seizette will take over unless we act. Mila must prove that the council has all the evidence they need and include the plan they wish to execute. Inevitably, the arguments must prove that their viewpoint will be the best course of action to cease the hostile takeover of Seizette and her kind. If the council fails, and the Head Councilor is replaced with Seizette or a monarch supporter, then Hyperion will most certainly be shut down, and any talk of changing one's colors or living a life different than that you were born to will be squashed."

"Let's not forget about all the humans that will suffer too," Nathanial added. "Being a factory without regulations is no picnic. Human hospitals are now at max capacity, thanks to the abuse of Grit-the-Gook-Whoa's new monopoly. People are being told to self-isolate to avoid spreading sickness. I can't even imagine what would happen if Seizette was given full control over the sprite world."

"Spaz, this is ridiculous." Mila rolled her eyes.

"What exactly do we get for winning this debate?" Nathanial asked, curious to see if Mila could prove the council's plan of action.

"If Nat wins, we go to the Head Councilor with the new evidence that he has gathered which proves Seizette's evil uprising. If Mila wins, we can relax, and"—Spassel smirked at Mila for his conclusion—"you get to tell Nat you told him so."

Aliya started clapping.

"You think this is a good idea?" Nathanial asked.

"Are you kidding me? It's great! I for one would

love to see who wins the debate. I hope it's Mila, no offense."

"No offense?" Nathanial moped.

Mila chortled.

"Well, if she wins it'd be a lot better for all of us, don't you think?" Aliya asked, her smile fading slightly. Everyone caught her meaning and sobered up a notch.

"Okay," Mila finally said. "I'm down. The end of the week isn't much time… for you, Nat. I mean, you need to find something new beyond 'the Swartza are scum,' because we already know that. You need to dig up some dirt that is so filthy that even Boss would act on it. Sure you can handle it?"

"Well, you have to do more than read people's minds, Mila. You need real evidence," Nathanial insisted.

"How about just a witness?" Spassel said. "We do this in teams. If two eavesdroppers overhear the same thing, it can be counted as evidence. Naturally, I'm rooting for Nat, so I should be with Mila to keep her straight. Sorry, Nat." As if this would disappoint Nathanial immensely. "So, Aliya, you'll have to be with Nat, since you are for Mila."

Everyone nodded. The game was afoot.

THE INTERPRETABLE TRUTH

It dawned on Nathanial the next morning that Mila was right about the tight schedule. How was he going to find time to spy and gather evidence for a presentation at the end of the week when he had classes and physical training every day? He expressed this concern to Aliya over the breakfast buffet, where Mila and Spassel were, suspiciously, nowhere to be found.

"We could just ask Boss how the meeting went last night," Aliya said, but Nathanial looked skeptical.

"When has Boss ever given me information that I asked for? Remember, this is the same guy who refused to tell me about you when I flat out asked him."

Aliya groaned. "What about Bunny? She's always been helpful."

"Yeah. If she knows anything, she's more likely to share," Nathanial thought aloud, "but she's not allowed in any of the meetings. We'll ask next time we see her, though."

In class, Nathanial's bewilderment at Mila and Spassel's continued absence was amplified. Were they really going to skip class to get their evidence? That seemed a little unfair. But it wasn't as though classes were like real school, anyway. It was nothing like Hyperion or Swartza High, more like an after-school program. There were only about fifteen kids in the complex who were school-age, after all. One sprite taught the entire group, from eight to eighteen years old.

Most of the adults at Sanctuary had sent their kids to relatives far away. The kids who were there had been sent by parents who feared that they would be used as leverage against them, parents in such high public view that it would be crazy to do anything directly to them personally. But kids had been going missing of late, and it always seemed to be those of pro-factory rights families.

Spassel's parents had wanted to join Sanctuary, but feared that they were being tracked. Mila's parents were proud of her rebellious spirit and were actively fighting Hyperion's shutdown while she remained safely hidden. Nathanial's mom thought that he was doing a student exchange program abroad, and Aliya's family most likely thought she had died long ago. It really felt like a band of misfit orphans.

"Maybe we should split, too," Nathanial whispered to Aliya. "We can't let Mila get the upper hand on us."

Ms. Colette, rose-cheeked as always, with glass sticks holding her pink, blue, and yellow lollypop bun atop her head, entered the room and shut the door behind her.

"Too late," Aliya whispered.

Nathanial straightened up. He had a natural respect for Ms. Colette that had struck him from the first time he saw her, months back. He felt like he knew her right away.

"Good morning, class," the teacher said with a faded French accent. She pushed up her red horn-rimmed glasses, which had a funny way of accenting the colorful unicorn eyeliner that pointed up and away from each eye's corner.

"Good morning, Ms. Colette," the students sang in unison.

"I hope you all had a nice weekend. And a quick congratulations to Nathan for doing so well getting that artifact yesterday. Receiving just one small mark at the end is not a small feat."

Nathanial pushed a smile onto his face and waved his thanks, but a twinge of embarrassment tugged at him. He didn't deserve congratulations unless there were no marks.

"I know we usually start with math on Monday mornings," Ms. Collette said, swiping the equations off the illuminated wall before them, "but after last night's new arrival—and seeing as many of you don't have anyone to turn to about what is going on in the world—I thought it'd be a good idea to give you all a small talk."

Nathanial's pointed ears perked. He couldn't believe his luck. Was he about to get fuel for his debate that Mila would miss out on?

"Most of you know we get our news largely from communal billboards and bulletins on tablets or traditional leaflet circulation. We never quite took to moving pictures the way humans did, even though we've had fun fiddling with their programing from time to time. Really, we're a word of mouth society, many of us too busy to read or even to be interested in what's going on outside of our own communities. So you can imagine everyone's surprise when someone showed up with one of these last night."

From behind her desk, Ms. Colette pulled up a mechanical device the size and shape of a 20oz thermos. Oval diamonds attached to several metal arms clung tight to the shiny cylindrical surface.

"They're calling it the Truth Seer."

"Who's calling it that?" Nathanial asked without

thinking.

"The authorities, apparently," Ms. Colette responded. "Though we have three council members staying here with us and they did not know about its distribution plans. Every major factory town now has one of these in their central courtyard."

"What does it do?" asked a small girl in the front row.

"Why don't we find out together? Would you like to volunteer, Aida?" Ms. Colette asked, with an encouraging smile.

The colorless nine-year-old Aida, half a dozen scrunchied pigtails on her head, stood and walked up to the device. "What do I do?"

"Tell me something that you would like to know about," Ms. Collette said.

"My parents are scared. They sent me here all by myself, and I don't know why."

"What do your parents do?"

"They used to be chairsprites of the board of Grit-the-Gook Pro, the factory friendly lysozyme company, before it shut down. Now they've been recruited to work for Big Lyso, making Grit-the-Gook-Whoa. That's when they got really scared and said I had to come here for protection."

"Okay," Ms. Colette said, "start by saying the

words 'Truth Seer,' and then just ask it what you'd like explained."

Aida licked her lips. "Truth Seer, can you tell me why my parents are scared to work for Grit-the-Gook-Whoa?"

The metallic arms of the device extended out from the central column. A blinding light shone through the crystals, creating momentary prisms throughout the room. Then someone Nathanial knew to be a very bad sprite appeared, standing in the front of the room.

"Hello," the deep green sprite said, with an attempted smile that came off as a grimace. He stood two heads taller than Ms. Colette, and his wide girth pushed the limits of his straining business attire. His bald head was toady and his pointed ears jagged. "I am Codfear Brack, Head Chair of Headquarters, and proud C.E.O of Grit-the-Gook-Whoa. I understand many felt afraid when the *pro-factory*"—he air quoted the words—"plants shut down recently. I'm here to address your concerns as a concerned citizen myself.

"This device you are using can only show you the truth. It is a collection of real memories. Even my own projection is a memory. But, because many of the viewpoints about to be shown to you are not from my own experiences, only my voice will accompany you, to help explain what you are seeing."

The room changed dramatically, so that the class sat in the center of a city that Nathanial recognized. He'd first entered it through the corner niche in his room.

The students gasped as their desks and chairs appeared to render themselves invisible. They simply floated, legs bent in the air, as the busy sprites went about their day, often passing right through them. One kid stumbled back out of his invisible chair and screamed as a fluffy-headed, bronze-faced sprite ran by to stop a squat sprite from digging in a trash bin.

"This was Thatcherville," the voice of Codfear Brack continued, sounding as if it came from just in front of them.

Nathanial gulped and looked to see if any of the students were staring at him. He was pretty sure that had been Bunny who'd just ran by. Were these his memories?

"Thatcherville is a prime example of the glory that can be accomplished with a strictly run factory. The profits were so great for so long that we put Headquarters in orbit above this factory's location."

The room shifted to a ghost town.

"And this is what happens to the richest city on the east coast when the factory demands negotiations." Codfear Brack spoke coldly.

Heat burned Nathanial's face and a lump formed in his throat. He'd seen the town like that just a year after he'd made his wish to become a sprite. The out of business signs boarding up shop windows. The Grit-the-Gook flyers littering the streets. The empty basket elevators to the sky-rise apartments. He'd felt guilty, but what was he supposed to have done? They were keeping him prisoner and profiting from his torture!

Nevertheless, the faces of the surrounding students expressed anger at the sight. Nathanial hoped they wouldn't find out it was him. Most of them already knew he was a changeling, a human turned sprite. He'd wanted to be open and honest about himself in this new place, and thought he'd be safe amongst the company of outcasts. But now that old fear of them judging him for his differences was creeping back in.

"This is why factory friendly producers can't stay afloat," Codfear Brack said as the classroom reappeared and the towering bulk of a sprite again stood before them. "Their cost of operating is higher, and their profits are not sustainable. But we at Big Lyso were happy to open our arms to those sprites who had nowhere to turn when their production went under. Please don't be afraid of this happy change. We are here to help you get through." With that, his image faded, the cylinder went dark, and the diamonds contracted back into their original state.

No one spoke for a few long seconds. Nathanial and Aliya looked at each other, wide-eyed.

"So," Aida tried to reason as she slowly took her seat, "my parents shouldn't be afraid then?"

Ms. Colette put the device back under the desk, stood in front of the class, and said with her hands tightly grasped in front of her. "This device is what we call political propaganda."

The barbed wire around Nathanial's stomach loosened a bit. Good. Ms. Colette wasn't buying it.

"This is one of the most dangerous weapons we have ever seen," she continued. "Images can be more powerful than the sword. Cut someone down and what do you have? A dead sprite that can do nothing for you, perhaps even a martyr who rallies more against you. *Change* someone's mind, however, and you've gained an ally who will not only work for you but who will fight for your cause and do so with their whole heart."

"But the Truth Seer shows things from memory. If it changes minds by showing the truth, then…

that's okay, right?" asked a slightly yellow boy from the back.

"Yes, that would be okay," Ms. Colette said, matter-of-factly. "But the truth with *omissions* or the truth accompanied by lies, is not okay. These memories you just saw were perfectly selected and paired with words to suit the agenda of Big Lyso. You saw a factory town that had been shut down, but it had nothing to do with factory friendly operations, as Codfear said. Your parents would not have sent you here if this was the clear truth, dear Aida. I've shown you this so that you can know why there have been no protests or uprisings in the cities. Our enemy is formidable because they are clever. We must outwit them. But don't worry, sweet ones. We've done it before."

The door opened and a brown, gangly sprite popped his head into the room. "Ms. Colette, may I speak with you?"

Ms. Colette nodded and held a finger up to him as she addressed the class. "Okay, class, you are dismissed for today. It seems you'll have some extra time to chat amongst yourselves before field practice."

All the kids hurried out of the room, the gangly sprite waiting anxiously for them to do so.

The chatter exploded almost immediately in the

hall. Nathanial took Aliya's arm to slow her into the back of the group.

"What are you thinking?" she asked as the class dissipated and divided into different halls.

Nathanial whispered, "I think those were my memories we just saw."

"What? How is that possible?"

"I was stuck in the diamond for a while when I failed Seizette's trials. That must have been all she needed to download my memories."

Aliya groaned. "Creepy."

He wavered momentarily, recalling Aliya's blood memories that he'd stumbled upon while in the diamond. He still hadn't found the right moment to tell her what he'd seen. He basically had secret knowledge that she was adopted. He wished he'd read some book on how parents told their kids they weren't their biological children, but then, he never knew he was going to need that kind of information.

"What is it?" Aliya asked.

"Oh. Uh, I was just thinking the Truth Seer would be great to have at the debate."

"I don't think that's something Ms. Colette can just hand over to a couple of students. It's seems pretty important," Aliya said.

"I know," Nathanial agreed. "But maybe we can

just borrow it and then return it right after the debate."

"Okay… but just in case we aren't able to *borrow* it, we should think of something else as a backup."

Nathanial moaned. It was like the clouds had opened with a gift from the debate gods and now he was back in the dark. "I don't have any other ideas," he admitted.

"We still have a week to come up with something. Let's just put the Truth Seer on the back burner for now."

Nathanial and Aliya parted ways to get suited up for field practice. Getting wrapped up in his armor wasn't too big a deal; he could just slip the gear on and tie a few strings. But removing the decorative dressings off his wings was a tricky process. He backed into a mount on the wall until it clicked, indicating alignment. Then he stepped away from the device that held tight to the cloth material, allowing it to peel off his wings so they no longer looked like coattails of his jacket. Now the bronze and silver graft was revealed. It had been incorporated into his wings to strengthen them after they'd first emerged, mangled and broken from an accident. He shook out his wings, folded them, checked the body-length mirror to watch them settle into their shield form, and was about to leave his room when he caught a glance of his pocket notebook.

He'd been writing in it so much that he'd come to the point where he'd expected the pages to run out. But like the fairy tale of the man who is gifted a purse that always has ten pieces of gold, so too Nathanial found new pages to fill each time he opened his notebook.

Nathanial picked up the bark-like book with the golden stitching that read *'All I need to know is within'* and pulled the glass pen from its spine. He flipped past pages with notes on tricks he'd learned and stories he'd discovered from the Crossing Treaty book he'd read in Swartza High, and things he'd seen while in the diamond.

He stopped momentarily on his drawn reproduction of Boss being cursed; recalling the watercolors of the Crossing Treaty book represented the moment more accurately, in contrast to what he was looking at in black and white. It had showed a bold golden warrior forcibly shrunk down into a sad blue slump of a being. He still hadn't brought this newfound knowledge up to Boss, and he wasn't sure there was much point. This curse of his, the nameless curse, made it very difficult for Boss to talk about his past. Nathanial wasn't even sure how much Boss could remember, and so Nathanial tried to be more lenient with Boss's secretive ways.

Flipping on to the next empty page, Nathanial placed the glass pen on its speckled surface and watched the dots coalesce into the image in his mind. The sketch formed into the Truth Seer, with the title over it, and a paragraph about what he had heard in class wrote itself underneath the image. When he was done, Nathanial set the book back on his bedside table and left the room.

THE MISFIT GAMES

During field practice, Nathanial's mind was so preoccupied with how to win his debate that he was an absolute blunder. He failed to dodge the roots that his training partner sent toward him, and then he got cocooned into a grass strand. Finally, Nathanial pleaded for a time out.

Boss and Phlegm had been watching him and looked to be debating which one of them should go talk to him. Boss uncrossed his arms and walked over to join Nathanial on the root bench he was seated on.

"What's going on?" Boss asked. "Are you really that upset about the mark yesterday?"

"What?" Nathanial had momentarily forgotten there was a yesterday. "Oh, no, I'm over that. I shouldn't expect to beat you. I don't know what I was thinking."

Boss's eyes widened and he kept momentarily silent before he said, "That doesn't sound like the competitive Nathanial that I know."

"I'm not competitive," Nathanial started to say,

but saw the smirk in Boss's eyes. "I prefer to look at it as trying my best."

"There's nothing wrong with it," Boss said. "It's good to have a competitive spirit. Don't let my being impossible to beat stop you from trying."

Nathanial couldn't help but laugh. "Right," he said, shaking his head. But his smile quickly faded. He wanted to confide in Boss, ask him what chance they had against Seizette. Or, rather, he wanted Boss to confide in him. He wished Boss would tell him what was going on in those top secret council meetings. He knew it was a long shot, but he aimed for it, anyway. "How did the council meeting go last night?"

Boss's attempt to pry out Nathanial's mood shifted quickly into shutdown mode. He gave a short answer: "Long."

"Long?" Nathanial repeated.

"Very," Boss added.

"I see," Nathanial said, without surprise for Boss's lack of detail. "Well, thanks for your concern but I'm fine." He got up and went to spar with his partner again.

After another hour, Nathanial had enough scrapes and bruises that he asked that his armor be examined for weak spots. He took another break and went over to see Aliya, bow training with a half dozen other sprites. Bunny, Gem, and Pat were a few of the older sprites, giving out pointers on how to hit their stuffed and whiskered targets, which stood far away. Pat had just congratulated Aliya on hitting square through an acorn that was a makeshift eye and was moving on to the next sprite.

"Still no Mila or Spassel," Nathanial said, giving Aliya such a fright her next arrow shot straight up into the air.

"Rogue arrow!" she shouted, pointing up. There were a couple of screams and everyone ran back. They watched as the arrow came down just feet in front of the training line. "Don't do that!" Aliya slapped Nathanial's arm.

"Ow," he said rubbing the abused spot. "I have a grass cut there."

Aliya pushed a loose strand of hair out of her face, picked the arrow out of the ground, and said, "I know, it's weird. No one has seen them all day."

"Do you think we should be worried?" Nathanial asked.

Aliya sighed. "I'm not sure yet."

"Okay, all you sharpshooters and grass slingers," Bunny called over the field. "Refuel time!"

"You heard her," Phlegm reiterated on the far side of the field. "That's lunch!"

"If Spassel isn't at lunch, then it's definitely time to worry," Nathanial said, herding along with the other trainees. "It was weird enough he missed breakfast."

Lunch was buffet style, much like breakfast had been, but instead of pastries and fruits there were stews, breads, and a battered assortment of bug legs. A vat of sparkling honey swirl spritzer sat at the end of the line, and Nathanial filled his cup to the brim. It was a mix of tree sap, honey, and flower dew that had been spiked with a kick from the nectar sprites.

Nathanial and Aliya took their trays to their usual alcove table and scanned the buffet line for any sign of their friends.

"I think we need to call out the hounds," Nathanial grumbled over the no shows.

"Wait," Aliya said, and sat up tall. "Look over there!"

At a distant corner table, Nathanial could just make out a white tuft of hair that was unmistakably Spassel. Almost unconsciously, Nathanial tiptoed, "Pink Panther"-style, to a nearer corner until he could make out Mila, too. Nathanial's jaw dropped. They were sitting with Larix and Amaranth. He had never seen Mila looking so delighted.

"Can you believe it?" Nathanial whispered, with

the assumption that Aliya was still next to him. But she had never left the table. He hurried back over and sat down. "Do you see who they're with?"

Aliya laughed. "Yes, and I don't have to look so obviously sneaky about it either."

"What do you think they're doing?"

"Gathering evidence for our debate, obviously," Aliya said.

"Wow, they went straight for the throat, didn't they?" Nathanial said, amazed at their gall. "I think the Truth Seer is our only chance."

Aliya bit her lip. "Look, I'm not saying it's not a good idea, but it won't be easy to get our hands on. It shouldn't be your only evidence, anyway. The council already knows about the Truth Seer, so they probably already have a plan to combat it. Let's think of something else."

Nathanial sighed. "I suppose you're right. But I still want to show them what the public is being fed. Just think of all the other questions we could ask it. If we know what the public thinks is the truth, then we'll know what we need to disprove."

"You have a good point," Aliya agreed.

Nearing the end of lunch, Mila finally waltzed over to Nathanial and Aliya while Spassel scurried over to the food options.

"Hello my beloved losers-to-be," Mila said,

leaning casually on the table.

"Oh look, Aliya, we were wrong," Nathanial said, pretending not to be phased. "They aren't dead. How overjoyed I am to see that you missed class for no reason."

"We had a much better reason than death to miss class!" Mila guffawed. "We were hanging out with the toughest sprite in town."

"Yeah, we saw you with Amaranth," said Nathanial. "So you already have all the evidence you need, then?"

"In the bag, like I said. Easy-peasy." Mila smirked and looked over to Spassel, who was sliding into the booth with a piled tray of grub.

"The evidence is pretty conclusive from our current explored standpoint," Spassel said, nodding apologetically toward Nathanial.

"Well, I've got some conclusive evidence from the class that *you* missed today, so, you know, don't be so sure of yourself," Nathanial retorted.

"You mean the Truth Seer?" Mila guessed. Nathanial gasped. "Yeah, we went to get permission from Ms. Colette to miss class. She gave us a personal demonstration of what the Truth Seer could do. You're going to need more than that if you want to win the debate, just a friendly head's up."

Aliya pursed her lips. She seemed disappointed on Nathanial's behalf, but also not surprised.

"Do you have any private lessons with Boss or Phlegm today?" Spassel asked Nathanial, trying to change the awkward subject.

"No," Nathanial said flatly. "They're giving me a night to mend. I got pretty banged up in the field today."

"Why?" Mila asked with almost true concern.

"Just wasn't feeling it," Nathanial answered shortly.

"Well, good!" Spassel perked up, then must have realized how that sounded, judging by his pained expression. "I mean, not good that you got hurt, but that we can join the Misfit Games."

"The Misfit Games?" Aliya asked, wrinkling her nose.

"Yeah! The kids have put together a game that incorporates the best parts of their hometown games. I hear it's mostly based off Hedgeball, but it's been modified so we're less likely to get hurt. What d'you guys think?"

"I don't know," Mila said, a glint behind her violet eyes. "Nat probably needs more time to research his evidence."

"He's doing well with his evidence." Aliya jumped in to defend Nathanial, taking everyone off guard. "I think we should play with the other kids. We all could use some fun."

Nathanial's heart fluttered. He'd been feeling uneasy about Aliya rooting for Mila in the debate. He secretly hoped Mila would crush it, but he also couldn't stand by and do nothing when he was so unsure about such a big deal. It was nice to have Aliya truly on his side at that moment.

After lunch, they met up with the self-proclaimed misfits. It wasn't just the fifteen kids from class, but also five fully-colored sprites in their early twenties who were clearly ready for some sport; all of them had padded up for the event. The only girl from the budding-adult group stepped forward with a seedball stick in hand. Nathanial recognized the sports gear from playing Hedgeball at Swartza High. It had a wide rope basket on the end of a long broom-like handle.

"Alright! What a great turn out for our first ever Misfit Games!" she said, beaming at the group. Her teal complexion was highlighted with bright turquoise around her eyes, which extended up and back into the two buns atop her head. "I'm Kia. I'll be one of the team captains. This is Onix. He'll be the other."

A burly fellow that looked like he'd been dipped in the last dye cup at Easter put his hand up in greeting. He had such a mix of splotches that there was no one defining color to his mostly-dark skin. His hair was buzzed short on one side, and the other had multiple tiny braids that came down to gather in a bunch under his pointed ear.

"I'll explain the rules we decided on shortly, but first, who here has an animal companion?" Kia asked, brows lifted.

Nathanial wasn't sure if he should raise his hand. He and Sidian wanted to be companions, but Boss had made it sound like it was a to-be-determined matter, even after all the training they'd done together. Mila didn't seem to agree with his uncertainty, however, and she forced his arm high into the air.

"Hey!" Nathanial started to protest but then let his arm remain in the air as he asked her, "What about you and Ori?"

"Ori's not mine," she said with a frown. "She's my mom's."

"Oh," Nathanial said.

Five others had their hands raised, and Kia asked them all to stand together behind her. "Now, if you could all call them for me, please," she added.

Nathanial cleared his throat and cupped his

hands. Where most the kids made grumbling, snooting, or twittering noises, Nathanial called, "Sidian!"

Two flying squirrels, a blue jay, a mouse, and a young fox all appeared from different parts of the woods until they came to rest around the kids beside Nathanial. He cleared his throat as he felt everyone's eyes falling upon him.

He was about to call for Sidian again when a giant shadow swooped over them. Sidian was coming in for a landing, and the hair on every sprite's head tussled fiercely in the wind beneath his wings. Nathanial had, by far, the largest companion there.

Sidian pushed his way between the gekkering fox and the chirping blue jay to let Nathanial pet his beak. Nathanial smiled apologetically to the owners of the unappreciative fox and blue jay.

"Wow," Kia said. "A raven. Huh."

Nathanial didn't see what the fuss was about. Why was everyone looking at him like that? Yeah, Sidian towered over the rest, but it couldn't be *that* odd.

"Anyway." Kia attempted to regain her composure. "We have two flyers, so one can go on each team. Onix, you want the raven?"

Onix looked just as perplexed to see Sidian as the rest, but quickly shook it off and said, "I'm always up for a challenge."

"Great, then I'll take the blue jay. A squirrel can go on each team—you guys decide—and I'll take the fox since you have the raven. That puts the mouse with Onix. Okay, now let's divide the rest of us by height."

It went on like this until the two teams were pretty evenly matched, at least according to Kia.

"Now I'll call the rest of the team," Kia said, putting two fingers in her mouth to form a loud whistle. A scurry of chipmunks rushed out from the trees. "Whoa, whoa, whoa!" she said, holding her hands up to the gathering. "I only need fourteen!"

Onix threw down a long bag that'd been slung across his shoulder. "Take a stick," he told the group, and they did.

"Everyone knows the rules of Hedgeball, right?" Kia asked the excited players around her. Everyone nodded.

Nathanial was always surprised when a sprite question was put forward that he actually knew the answer to. It was almost like he belonged. But he also hoped that Spassel was right when he said this game was only *like* Hedgeball. He didn't feel much like getting battered by sticks when he was already sore from training. At least there were no hedgehogs; that eliminated the threat of quill impalements.

"The elements we've kept from Hedgeball are the sticks for passing the ball to teammates and the flowering of arches for most of the scorekeeping." The older sprites were making roots sprout up around the field and bending them into arches as Kia continued. "We don't have ramps since we didn't want the hedgehogs that would use them for speed boosts, but that gave Dusty an idea to add something from a game he plays back home. Dusty, do you want to explain?"

The boy by the blue jay, eyes and hair the color of sand, said, "Yeah, back home we all have blue jay companions and we play a game called Block Blue where the scoring goals are just one on each side of the field. The ball is passed bird-to-bird down the field and you have to try to get the ball past a Blocking Blue and into the opposing team's basket to score."

Nathanial thought it sounded a bit like basketball.

"So," Kia picked back up, "we're cutting down the number of arches from regular Hedgeball to just nineteen and adding a high-basket hoop at each end of the field. I'm sure it will take everyone some time to get the hang of how to chuck the ball into the basket from your seedsticks net, but I assure you it's possible. We tested it out.

"Also, it takes multiple shots to flower the hoop basket completely, and the team to accomplish it first gets double points. That means that the team that gets the most arches bloomed doesn't necessarily win, if the other team finishes their basket hoop first. The game ends when all arches are flowered and each team has at least one basket hoop. Dusty will be the blocker of one hoop, and the raven can block the other."

"You can call me Nathan," Nathanial said, realizing they hadn't been introduced and preferring to use a name he felt was more his own while at Sanctuary. He didn't mind that Spassel and Mila still called him Nat, but the buggy nickname wasn't something he wanted to spread further than that.

"Great. Nice to meet you, Nathan. Do you have any questions about blocking?"

Nathanial shook his head, but his stomach was feeling nervous. "I think I'll work it out as we go along." He foresaw lots of seedballs coming at him in his near future.

Onix pulled the seedball out of a bag, hopped onto a chipmunk the equivalent size of a monster truck, and said, "Let's do this already. We'll all be learning as we go."

Kia threw a green dust bag around, saying, "Pepper your animals and sticks to form your team color."

Nathanial caught a red bag from Onix and dusted his net. The entire stick changed from white to red.

"Wait. Why do I need a stick if I'm only blocking?" Nathanial asked Onix.

Dusty gave him his answer. "If you catch the seedball in your net, that gives you a chance to steal. You can fly down to my side and see if you can score. It's very risky, though, because if I catch it, I can throw it down the field to a team member who then has a chance at your wide-open goal."

"Wow, okay." Nathanial thought about it. "Can I just pass it to one of my team members instead?"

"You can." Dusty shrugged. "Okay, let's get this show on the road!" Dusty whooped and flew off to his side of the field.

"You ready for this?" Nathanial asked Sidian.

Sidian cawed and clicked excitedly. Nathanial peppered Sidian and watched him turn red. It was a pretty awesome sight, and Nathanial couldn't help but get excited as well.

DROPPING THE BALL

Once the seedball had been coated in pollen by a sprite-sized bee and dropped into the bumper car fray of chipmunks below, Nathanial was left to take his cues from watching Dusty at the other end of the field. Dusty kept his blue jay perched on top of the basket until the opposing team got close with the seedball. Then he'd swoop down to fly between them and the basket in case they tried to shoot for it.

Kia had advised her team to concentrate on the arches first, and Sidian was getting kind of bored. Nathanial was continuously readjusting to keep centrally seated between the shifting shoulder blades that were begging for action. Green and red flowers burst out all over the place, but not one seedball had come to threaten him and Sidian yet.

Nathanial liked watching how competitive Aliya and Mila were being. They'd been placed on opposite teams, and Aliya was on his. It really ruffled Mila's feathers when Aliya stole the seedball right out from under her. He laughed out loud.

Then Nathanial noticed a change in tactics forming on the field. Red had the upper hand in arches, which meant that if green wanted a chance to win, they would need to start making some baskets.

"Okay, Sidian, get ready. I think we're about to see some action."

Sure enough, the greens had the seedball and were stampeding his way. Nathanial and Sidian took flight. It almost seemed unfair at first, with Sidian having such a large wingspan. He didn't see how the ball could get past it. But as the ball flew towards him, he fumbled it away with his clumsy stick and his disadvantage became apparent. It seemed almost impossible to catch the seedball past the bulk of Sidian. It made it so the greens could take several more shots before the reds swept the seedball back away down the field.

Sidian returned to his perch above the basket. "Phew!" Nathanial caught his breath. "That got crazy quick."

Sidian cawed, expressing how well he'd done blocking the last basket.

"Yeah you blocked the basket, but I couldn't catch that seedball for the life of me. I don't think we're ever going to steal a goal."

Sidian clicked and twisted his head. On the

other side of the field, Nathanial was awestruck over how the pro goalkeeper managed it. Dusty swooped down with the speed and agility of his small blue jay and caught the seedball in his net.

"Oh, boy. Here we go!" Nathanial yelled, patting Sidian's neck, and they took flight again.

Dusty was heading right for them with a gigantic smile on his face.

"Get ready," Nathanial encouraged his counterpart.

Nathanial could feel Sidian's excitement running through him. His heart tripled its drumbeat. His eyes sharpened on the seedball. Then, in a confusing blur of events, he and Sidian moved to block Dusty, but he steered his blue jay up and around, passing right overhead. Dusty slammed his net against the open goal basket and the seedball shot through its cornucopia shape to exit back down into the fray of teammates below.

Nathanial felt Sidian's frustration and had to shake the unnerved feelings apart from his own before he could try and calm his companion down. "It's okay," Nathanial said. "It's okay. This is our first time playing. Dusty has loads of experience on us."

Nathanial patted Sidian's head, but the bird's neck feathers stayed ruffled.

Unfortunately, the game continued in this manner. Dusty scored a few more times, and each time Sidian became more and more flustered. The flowers of their goal post were riddled in green, down to the last few lengths. It appeared Dusty only needed one more shot to win it for his team.

"Come on, Nathan!" yelled Onix from below. "You've got to steal us some goals or we're done for!"

"Okay!" Nathanial said, getting his head in the zone. "We can do this, Sid. Next time the ground team tries to shoot a goal at us, just tuck in, drop down, and I'll have my net ready for the catch."

Sidian short-cawed and shuffled his shoulders. He was ready, and the greens were on their way towards them.

This was it. This was their chance. Mila lifted her green stick in the air and the seedball flew right toward them. Nathanial and Sidian moved as one; it was like Nathanial was an extension of Sidian. Within a moment of Nathanial catching the seedball, Sidian swooped toward the opposite goal.

Nathanial grinned broadly as he approached Dusty. Dusty looked ready, and anticipation crackled in the air. But suddenly, something was wrong. His rival's good humor fell into fear, and then everything slowed. Numbness trickled over Nathanial. He realized he was not in control.

Sidian reached out his claws and Nathanial ached at the disbelief in Dusty's eyes. The blue jay was wrapped up into the raven's talons, Sidian twisted around and Nathanial's stick contacted with the basket. The seedball rolled through and landed with a hard *thunk* onto the ground.

Sidian landed in celebration. He scratched the ground and bobbed his head. It took an immense amount of will power for Nathanial to gain control over his own limbs and jump off Sidian. He moved slowly, over to where the small blue jay had been thrown.

"Dusty," Nathanial called, his voice tight. The bird's head and back, where Dusty had cheerfully ridden just moments before, was turned away and unmoving. "Dusty, are you okay?"

The older sprites finally arrived from across the field and rushed past Nathanial. They gathered around the far side of the blue jay. Onix pulled Dusty out from underneath the bird. There was a groan. Relief flooded Nathanial, only for it to disappear as soon as it'd come. Scornful eyes looked his way.

"Is he okay?" Nathanial took another baby step closer. "Is the blue jay…?" He couldn't finish.

Onix was half-carrying a dazed Dusty back toward Sanctuary.

"Jade." Dusty's groans finally became understandable. "Jade." Dusty lifted his head and looked back at his bird. He pulled away from Onix and rushed back screaming. "Jade!" He slid down by the bird's side and put his hand on its beak. He bit back his stream of tears and, with a deep breath, concentrated on his blue jay.

Everyone stayed still and watched. Nathanial felt helpless.

"It's okay," Dusty finally said, and everyone took a breath. "She'll be okay. Just knocked out."

Then Dusty's attention turned on Nathanial, all of his hate apparent in the sand storm that brewed in his eyes as he stood. "What were you thinking?"

"What... I..." Nathanial stammered. "I think Sidian just got carried away. I'm sure he didn't mean..."

"What could you possibly have been thinking?" Dusty asked again, moving toward Nathanial, a wild wind suddenly jostling his hair.

"I'm sorry," Nathanial tried to say. "It was an accident."

"Who chooses a raven for a companion?" Dusty pushed Nathanial backward with a gust of wind that emanated from his chest.

The older sprites rushed to pull him back.

"What?" Nathanial barely caught himself from falling. He hadn't expected someone from Sanctuary to use their blood abilities against him like that.

"Only the Swartza use ravens!" Dusty yelled. "And everyone knows they can't be trusted. Only a spy would pick a raven. Are you a spy?"

"No… I… no," Nathanial stammered once again.

Aliya, Mila, and Spassel quickly formed a defensive line around Nathanial.

"This raven is a rebel," Mila barked. "He left the Swartza. He thinks they're just as crazy as we all do. Sidian just needs to be re-trained, is all. It was an accident."

Nathanial's head buzzed. Sidian nudged him in the back.

"He doesn't belong here!" Dusty insisted, tears burning in his eyes. The wind died down as his rage turned to sorrow. "You can't re-train something that's been reared to kill. He should leave before he permanently hurts one of us." Dusty pulled away from his blockade and returned to his blue jay. He blanketed himself over her neck and let himself cry as he petted her.

Nathanial turned to Sidian and stroked his

beak. "You should go," he said softly. Sidian cawed and clicked. "I know. It's just better if you go right now."

Sidian nudged against Nathanial's chest one more time, then took off into the trees.

Nathanial walked back solemnly toward Sanctuary Hill. Aliya, Mila, and Spassel followed a few paces behind, the rest of the sprites staring after them.

Nathanial didn't feel up for a lengthy multi-course dinner that night. He picked up some bread to take back to his room and tried to assure his friends he was fine, but it was apparent the shock hadn't worn off. He ate the bread absentmindedly, sitting on his bed and staring into space.

When he finally went to sleep, it was plagued by a reoccurring nightmare. It always began with the nausea of being on a pirate ship in the middle of an ocean storm. Cyron, the broad-shouldered, thick-lipped, troll of a sprite whose colors were of the open sea, stood stonily in front of Nathanial, the dark splotches over his sharp cheekbones emphasizing the black well of hate in his eyes. He brought his giant hand down onto Nathanial's face and crumpled him to the ground.

When Nathanial could see again, he was still on the floor, but with Aliya sleeping in his arms. Seizette stood over him, blood in her smiling teeth.

"Please help her," Nathanial said. "She could die."

"I have contained the curse," the sultry voice responded, and blood trickled down her white shimmering neck. "For now." The echoing addition rang so loudly that the diamond walls around them cracked.

Nathanial sat up in bed, still seeing Seizette's cold look of control lingering in the darkness of his room.

"No," Nathanial whispered defiantly. "She won't reactivate the curse." It was something he told himself every night, but something he didn't believe. They had left Swartza High, and that was surely enough for Seizette to give Aliya's life back over to the blood curse, a punishment that had been handed down from her mother for leaving Seizette's service so long ago.

Nathanial laid back down, curling into his hot covers. He needed to find a way to stop the blood curse, just in case. Just to ease his mind, if nothing else. Thankfully, there was someone at Sanctuary who was always glad to help. He contented himself knowing that he was not alone and drifted back to sleep.

GATHERING EVIDENCE

When Nathanial woke, it was with the excitement of knowing he would be seeing Bunny soon. She was always up for sharing information, and he'd see her at field practice. He had the difficult task of remaining patient until then, though. He was too quiet at breakfast for Aliya's liking; she kept asking him what he was thinking. And then he was fidgety through their class on beetle herding.

When the teacher finally dismissed class, Nathanial jumped to his feet and close to sprinted out of the room. This threw him off-kilter when Aliya yanked him around the first corner they came to and brought them both to a sudden halt.

"What are you doing?" Nathanial asked.

"Let's get the Truth Seer," she said in a whisper, and peeked her head around the corner to see Ms. Colette disappearing down the hall.

"Really?" Nathanial asked, his eyebrows almost disappearing into his hairline.

"Yeah," she said pulling them back toward the

classroom, his hand in hers.

They snuck in and went straight for the desk. It wasn't there. Not under it, or in any of the drawers, or even in the chair that Nathanial inspected as a last resort.

"Where is it?" Nathanial griped.

"You won't find it in here," came a voice from the doorway. Nathanial and Aliya jumped around in fright. But it was just Mila, standing boldly with that deep maroon smile of hers. "It belongs to Amaranth. She just let Ms. Collette borrow it. It's probably back in her room."

"Let's go there, then," Aliya said.

"Why are you all of a sudden so into this idea?" Nathanial asked.

"Well, I agree with what you said yesterday. It'd be great to have it as evidence," Aliya explained, but it was clear she was holding back. Nathanial waited until she finally added, "And, okay, I'd love to ask it more questions. Because, well, see, I've been talking to Jozy."

"What? How?" Nathanial asked. "Isn't she still at Swartza High? That's a lockdown school. No way to call in or out."

Aliya held up her wrist, showing off her bracelet. It was made from all sorts of twisted strings that had an iridescent glow when the light caught it.

"A friendship bracelet," Mila said. "Neat trick. Two-way communication. Small enough to be overlooked by the Swartza but powerful enough to work long distance. Smart girl, that Jozy."

"Yeah, and she says Seizette just made it immediately mandatory for every student to take the diamond trials. Jozy just knows Seizette will find her heart lacking in the Swartza cause. The kids are being filtered through in such a frenzy her turn will come soon."

"Why would she force this right now?" Nathanial asked. "She used to let students take it in their own time. They did it by choice."

"Jozy thinks it's because of the vote that's coming up. Seizette wants to parade her best, brightest, and boldest school children to the assembly being held at Mount Lassen. A way to show off and gather support without actually telling anyone what happens to the kids that didn't make the cut. I want to ask the Truth Seer what happens to sprites that fail Swartza High. I'm sure it will give some sort of positive twist to the reality, something better than 'they get trapped in the diamond for reconditioning.' It'd be good to know what the public thinks is happening, and maybe I can find something to help Jozy."

"Well, good luck sneaking into Amaranth's

room," Mila said.

"Maybe you could ask her for it?" Nathanial suggested.

"Why would I do that?" Mila asked.

"Ugh," Nathanial grunted. "You know if I win the debate it won't just be for the pleasure of proving you wrong. It'll mean the adults are missing something that we can help them with. It could make the difference in defeating Seizette."

"If you find something out that the adults don't already know, I've got your back. Until then, may the best evidence win." Mila waved goodbye and left the classroom.

"Can you believe her?" Nathanial shook his head.

"I say we just go to Amaranth's room." Aliya headed toward the door. "I saw her go in there last night after dinner. I think I can get us in."

Aliya led Nathanial down a corridor he had never seen before. Unlike most of the mole-scooped hollows in Sanctuary, this hall was refined. The floor was glossy, the ceiling shone with glass light fixtures, and the walls had Romanesque pillars half-buried in them for aesthetic appeal.

"This has to be the hall of delegates," Nathanial said, impressed. "What brought you all the way down here last night?"

"You went to bed early, so I did the spying for the both of us," Aliya whispered. "I heard Amaranth talking to a delegate about the upcoming vote. I couldn't hear much, but there was something strange about the way they were speaking. It seemed more like scheming. I don't know. Mila would kill me if she heard me talking like this about her idol, but I think Amaranth is worth looking into."

"So we shouldn't just ask her for the Truth Seer, then." Nathanial bit his lip. "I hate stealing."

"I remember." Aliya smirked. He knew she was thinking of the time she'd goaded him into stealing some clothes to disguise themselves as sprites. Luckily, Bunny had found them and paid for some appropriate clothes on their behalf. "But we're just *borrowing* it, anyway." She was picking on him: he'd meant to *borrow* it from Ms. Colette all along.

With breaths held, they came to golden doors. Each door had different intricate etchings of utopian scenery, but as Nathanial examined the one before him, there was one crucial thing missing: a doorknob.

"Should we knock? What if she's in there?" Nathanial crinkled his nose.

"The delegates are in a meeting. We should be safe," Aliya said. "And I know how to get us in.

They're coded, see?" She pushed on the tip of a golden grape. It locked into place. Then she twisted a protruding flower until it clicked. Lastly, she pushed onto the edge of a bench a laughing sprite was sitting on until the other end of it popped out. She pulled the bench and the door opened.

"Nice!" Nathanial said, impressed. They hurried in and shut the door behind them.

The room was draped in purple silk. Jeweled traveling trunks lined the walls. Royal carpeting blanketed the floor, and elegant gowns hung along a dressing divider by an arched window.

"Wow," Aliya said. "I thought Amaranth was just a delegate for the Skilla, not the queen of Sheba."

Nathanial snorted. "Lots of trunks to look through."

"Better do it fast, then," Aliya said, heading for the one nearest her.

They opened all six trunks and proceeded to sort through them without making it obvious that they had done so.

"Anything?" Nathanial asked, picking up a pair of boots and looking under them at another pair of boots.

Aliya sighed. "Mainly just clothes."

Nathanial glanced around and saw that the

sunlight caught a glint under the bed. He ran over to it and pulled out a chest. Opening it like it was a pirate's long-lost booty, he found the Truth Seer inside. It was hugged tightly within a velvety fitted cushion.

"It's here!" Nathanial called to Aliya, who ran over.

Nathanial lifted the Truth Seer to reveal a pull string beneath it.

"There's something under here," Aliya said, and pulled the string, which removed the velvet holster. A maple wooden box was revealed. When she picked it up, another box was under it. She opened the one in her hand: ten diamonds, the exact size and shape of the ones in the Truth Seer, lined up in two rows of five.

"Huh," Aliya said as she picked one up. "Replacement parts, maybe?"

"Yeah, like backups. Maybe hard drives," Nathanial thought aloud.

"We should take them all, just in case." Aliya opened her messenger bag and put all three wooden boxes from Amaranth's chest into it.

Nathanial wrapped the Truth Seer into a scarf that was dangling off the bedpost. It was one of a dozen, and he didn't think it'd be missed. He carefully placed the protected Truth Seer on top of the thin boxes in Aliya's bag.

They quickly put everything back the way they'd found it and rushed to the door. Aliya put her ear to it.

"Sounds quiet," she said, and opened it slightly. "Looks clear. Let's go!"

They sped-walked through Sanctuary and out onto the field as if they had a fire sprite on their heels.

Nathanial blew out an anxiety-ridden breath. "I can't believe we just did that."

"I know. Let's just keep it secret until we can return it after the debate. Mila would probably tattle just to win."

Nathanial nodded. "Agreed. I only hope Amaranth won't notice it missing before then. I don't want her coming down on us with her mind-probing Skilla ways."

"Right. We should see what information we can get out of it right after field practice. Just in case."

Nathanial tried to put the Truth Seer on the back burner and refocus. He'd been looking forward to field practice so he could talk to Bunny. He spotted her with Gem some yards away, in the center of the training field. They looked to be showing Aida how to use a blade of grass like a whip. Bunny kept flicking Phlegm in the backside, then turning away like she hadn't done a thing.

Nathanial was heading her way when Spassel ran up in a twitter. "Hey, you guys! What are you up to?" he asked perkily.

"Nothing," Nathanial and Aliya said, too much in unison.

Spassel didn't falter. "Hey, Nat, I've got some buzz going on about the debate. I think all the kids from class will be there for sure, and maybe some of the older sprites too!"

"What?" Nathanial shouted, mouth agape.

"Yeah, isn't it great? After that disaster with Sidian yesterday there were some rumors at dinner that you were a Swartza spy, so I had to tell them that you were quite the opposite and even a keen advocate for taking action against the Swartza and that if they didn't believe me they could come see for themselves this Friday!"

"Oh, man," Nathanial groaned, slapping a hand to his face.

Mila ran over. "Did you give them the good news?"

"Just did!" Spassel said.

"How is that good news?" Nathanial asked, scanning the field of sprites-in-training that he was now threatened to be embarrassed in front of. "I don't want to debate in front of the whole class!

Most of them hate me after yesterday."

"Oh, they don't hate you." Mila waved the statement away. "They just don't trust you. All the more reason you should want to prove yourself. But I still plan to kick your butt. It's the perfect opportunity to let everyone know the situation is under control."

The twist in Nathanial's stomach was becoming a relentless knot. Not only was he sure to fumble in front of a crowd, but this also elevated the risk of Amaranth finding out they had her Truth Seer.

"Isn't there something you all should be doing?" Boss asked on approach, having just broken free from his dispersing class of sword trainees. "Like, oh, I don't know, practicing?"

"Sorry, Boss!" Spassel squeaked, and ran back to the obstacle course for his jumping lessons.

Nathanial and Aliya headed toward Bunny while Mila went to join the javelin team. Boss stopped Nathanial by clapping him on the shoulder. "Come here for a sec."

Aliya picked up on the private nature of the conversation and continued on.

"What's up?" Nathanial asked.

"How are you doing?" Boss inquired.

"Fine," Nathanial automatically responded.

"I heard about what happened with Sidian

yesterday," Boss said, narrowing his eyes.

"Oh. I know it was horrible, but I promise you he didn't mean to," Nathanial said quickly.

"He didn't mean to? That seems odd. How do you accidentally throw somebody to the ground?"

"Well, he said he knew he didn't kill them, that he knows the pressure he would have to squeeze for that to happen, and he only used half that pressure, but I told him it was wrong and he felt… well, he felt…" Nathanial searched for the words and didn't want to look Boss in the eyes.

Boss sighed. "Maybe it isn't such a good idea to let him train as your companion."

"No, Boss, really, you can't do that! He's trying. If you send him away that would crush him. Not only that, but he would be in danger. He's one of us!" Nathanial insisted.

"I'm not sure we can trust him," Boss said.

The words rang in Nathanial's ears as reflections upon himself. Mila had just said the students didn't trust him; that they thought he was a spy. They had every right to think that. If they knew the Swartza had tried to recruit him months before, they would surely burn him at the stake.

"Give him another shot," Nathanial said wholeheartedly.

Boss looked to be considering the implications

of his next words. "Okay," he finally said. "Only one more shot, though. We can't have distrust among us in these tense times. He needs to prove himself, and quickly. Show us that he's okay with you being in charge. Not the other way around."

"I understand. Thank you. I'll tell him. He'll do better," Nathanial said as he walked away and made a beeline for Bunny.

BUNNY'S MOLE HOLE

Nathanial pulled Bunny aside and said he wanted to talk to her about the battle blade in private. She'd been the one who had given it to him and was happy to agree to the talk. They went into her little "mole hole," as she liked to call it. Nathanial waited in her cozy, earthy, domed living room while she went to fetch them some honey juice from the kitchen.

The walls were tacked with fun and colorful posters that looked like travel brochures. They were unlike any Nathanial had seen before, because it was for an idea that no one in the sprite world would do and no one in the human world would believe possible: they were advertising epic adventures that took humans and sprites alike through the worlds of the big and small. Using her dust, Bunny promised things like taking the human's elevator up to the top of the Eiffel Tower and then shrinking the tour group down to eat at the prestigious sprite restaurant nestled within a desk inside the funny apartment way up there.

The drawing of the historical human wax figures towering around the tiny sprite restaurant looked like a unique experience for sure.

"Dust Bunny Tours. Where no adventure is too big or small," Nathanial read aloud. "Awesome."

Bunny came cheerfully into the room and handed Nathanial an opened bottle with a label that read "Sprigs Honey Juice."

"Thanks," he said, and took a scrumptious swig. "I love these posters." He pointed to the one in front of him. It was a concept drawing of people and sprites floating down Niagara Falls in a pod strung up to a leafy glider. "Have you been able to do any of these tours yet?"

"I took Gem on one, to test it out. That one there, to Petrified Forest." She pointed to a poster of a tree stump. Its age rings were crystalized into shades of red, blue, pink, and yellow. "She said it was amazing to be able to walk along the human trail and see so many of the different tree formations in such a short time. Then to shrink down inside one of them for lunch made her appreciate the details of nature that much more, to be able to see it from two perspectives. I think it was a good first go, but I won't know the real success of it until I can do it with a human/sprite mix. The whole point is to show the groups how we aren't so different, and just how much of the world we can all appreciate together if given the chance."

"That's the best, Bunny. I want to go on one of these tours with you. And, you know, I've been trying to figure out a way to tell my mom I'm a sprite. This sort of thing would blow her mind, in a good way. We could be your first human/sprite test group." Nathanial crinkled his nose with a sudden thought. "Bringing humans on these trips isn't like, you know, illegal is it? Didn't the Crossing Treaty prevent humans from ever being allowed to see sprites ever again?"

"Oh, Natey, my man, I'm so glad you brought that up! At first I was only going to take sprites into the human world with my dust company, very much assuming the same as you, that there had to be a law against including humans. But then, because of you, I did some research on it, and get this: it's actually not technically illegal to take the trick off a human's eyes! The Crossing Treaty just standardizes the widespread trick on human eyes to stop them from seeing us, so we don't have to negotiate with them when working on them as factories. It doesn't say it's removal is illegal when circumstances allow it.

"And that brings me back to how your handsome self inspired this thought. As I'm sure you remember, my dear sister took the trick off your eyes to stop Boss and Phlegm from working on you to grant your ten year wish to be well! My company will work on those same guidelines. Most of the humans that will be whisked away on my adventures will be sent to me by my connections with the wish sprites."

Nathanial smiled giddily, imagining the blast he and his mother would have on a Bunny-led tour. "Wow, Bunny! I can't wait to see this become a reality. My mom has been wanting to travel for so long, I'm just sure we can manage something to make this work for us."

He continued to scan the posters in awe when his eye caught on a depiction of a blue sprite fashioned in pirate gear next to a large three-masted sailing ship.

"Is that Boss with the *Argosy*?" he asked, surprised.

"Oh, yeah," Bunny giggled. "He used to buy my dust and turn all human-y to visit that port town all the time. I got the feeling he was looking for someone, but that darned curse of his probably just had him searching aimlessly. When I was drawing my concept tour for a unique trip into the past, he just naturally popped into my head. You know, I even think he worked your factory just to live in that headquarters' town. It had a direct tunnel that landed really close to that funky time bubble. Well, you remember the one."

Nathanial nodded and scrunched his brow in thought at this revelation. He vaguely remembered Bunny mentioning Boss's exploits into the human world before, but it'd totally slipped his mind.

Bunny took a seat and Nathanial followed. Her armchair was patched together with textured fabrics in a variety of colors. The couch Nathanial wiggled into reminded him of the blue monster from a kid's movie. It even had purple spots along the arms.

"So, is the battle blade doing something funky?" Bunny asked. "I was expecting it to do that sooner or later. What's it up to, exactly?"

Nathanial crinkled his brow. He had been going to ask what she knew about the blood curse, he just hadn't wanted to say anything worrisome in front of Aliya. But now his curiosity was piqued.

"Um, I'm not sure," Nathanial pondered. "What sort of things were you expecting?"

"Well," Bunny mused, "when I tapped the thing for you, while you were human, I thought I might have over-juiced it a bit. I told Boss back at Hyperion when you started showing off some extra oomph-y abilities that your new sprite vibrations were probably getting a kick from my own. I expected it to come through your battle blade, too, but you seemed to be handling it well. Not at all like the old folklore on the blades tells it."

"Old lore?" Nathanial repeated.

Bunny moved to the edge of her seat and put on a whispery voice. "Yeah, like, hundreds of years ago, the sprites forged the battle blades and paired them with great generals of the human world, giving the sprites who controlled the tap within the blades the power to direct our migration into new lands.

"Until one sprite fell head over heels in love with the general she'd been tasked with. That, of course, was considered a no-no, so she drastically faked their deaths, turned him into a sprite, and they disappeared into lore forever."

Nathanial's eye's widened. Was it possible she was talking about Seizette and General Grantz? He pictured the frozen form he'd seen, screaming as if in battle atop the giant winged bear, ominous even encased in the diamond at Swartza High.

"If she successfully faked their deaths, how does anyone know this story?" Nathanial asked.

"Well, I think that's why it's just lore, right? It's a story that's been romanticized. History shows a general and his paired sprite go missing and someone else makes up the love story about them running off together. But there's more: supposedly, when the general was turned into a sprite, the sprite's tap mingled with his blossoming vibrations, and it provided him with abilities that had never been seen before. He grew drunk on his endless power and killed his love in an uncontrollable psychotic episode that flattened an entire town!"

Nathanial gulped. Probably not Seizette, then. But still maybe Grantz?

"So, are you feeling like having a psychotic episode at all lately?" Bunny asked with a huge smile.

"Oh, yeah. But nothing as bad as that," Nathanial joked with the wave of his hand.

Bunny laughed.

"It does remind me of something Seizette said to me back at Swartza High, though," Nathanial said.

"Oh, yeah? What's that all-important inflated balloon got to say about it?"

Nathanial giggled. "She said if I didn't pick a sprite path soon that my vibrations would be in such turmoil that they could rip me apart."

"What?" Bunny reared back. "That's a load of baloney. Even Gem says the opposite. It's the fact that you *haven't* picked what type of sprite you want to be that's giving your vibrations the opportunity to shape themselves in whatever manner you care about."

"That's a relief to hear," he said, and let himself feel happy for a moment. Then he thought of how Seizette claimed she was the only one who could help him reach his potential, because she was the only one with changeling experience. "I have been wondering what I'm capable of, though. I'm not sure Boss can help me much past swordplay."

"Yeah," Bunny agreed. "Turning humans into sprites was mainly a wish sprite thing that became heavily regulated during the Third Rebellion. It's kind of new territory for all of us now, but that's what makes it fun. You don't have to go by other people's ideas of how you should be you. Experiment, you know? Especially with the battle blade. Feel it out. Let your vibrations be your guide."

Nathanial nodded. Neither Bunny nor Boss had ever mentioned General Grantz having a battle blade. He wondered if it was something he should share now but didn't like the implications of being so similar to Grantz. Seizette had never actually mentioned the battle blade, either. Maybe she and Grantz weren't the ones from the story, anyway. It had happened such a long time ago.

"How long is a typical sprite lifetime?" Nathanial asked.

"Well, now, that depends," Bunny said, and tapped her pointer finger on her cheek. "I'm sure you've figured out that most sprites are tied to the elements: fire, water, earth, and air are your basics, but our blood abilities have adapted to fill all sorts of roles. That mostly correlates to how long we live. Some of us are made of stronger stuff, or some just use less energy. Take Larix, for instance. He's one of the oldest sprites I know. Sometimes he just plants himself into a tree and lives off sunlight for, like, a decade at a time!"

"Whoa," Nathanial said. No wonder he looked part tree!

"But he's a rare example, I suppose. On average, I'd say your normal working-class sprite lives comfortably for about one hundred years."

"That's still a long time," Nathanial said, his eyes widening.

"Yeah, but remember there's the century families, too. They get an upper hand because they live two or even three times as long. They have more time to grow wealth and power. Then they pass their empires to their children, who do the same. You can see why they tend to develop big heads."

"What about Seizette?" Nathanial blurted. He couldn't help it. The curiosity was stirred. "How old is she?"

"Hmmm." Bunny scrunched her face in thought. "She's real old, ancient even. I don't know how she's managed to stay around for so long, really. Her diamond skin surely has something to do with that. Her kind are really rare, too. Could be why she's so grumpy. No one to get close to."

"What do you mean? Seems like plenty of sprites want to get close to her." Nathanial was thinking about how many of the Swartza he'd encountered who'd seemed to be infatuated with Seizette.

"At face value, it kind of makes sense. The long-lasting century-class sprites prefer to marry their own kind because it's hard to lose a life partner. Staying within your own class means you'll likely live long lives together, and it avoids the heartache that would come from falling for a sprite who lives only half as long. It seems logical, until you realize that the heart wants what it wants and doesn't always follow social cues. Makes it tough on a high society diamond sprite like Seizette who's lived longer than anyone I know and would only want a life partner of the highest standard." Bunny clicked her tongue and shook her head. "She must be very lonely."

Nathanial bit his lip. It was almost cause to feel sorry for Seizette—but no amount of loneliness should drive the sort of destruction Seizette craved. "So how many sprites today were actually alive during the Third Rebellion? Like, a majority, or…?"

"Eh, I know why you're asking that. Boss is always saying no one wants a Fourth Rebellion because plenty remember the Third, right?"

Nathanial nodded and set his empty bottle on the stalactite side table.

"Yeah, it's not a majority, but the stories are still fresh from just a couple of generations. My mother wasn't involved, but my mother's mother was."

"Wow." The puzzle pieces that formed his fragmented picture of the Third Rebellion were finally coming together. "Does that mean that sprites like Boss and Amaranth belong to century families?"

Bunny put her finger in the air with an, "Aha!" Her eyes sparkled. "Now you're starting to see why classifying people into groups is so pointless. Yes, they're from century families. They live a long time, but that doesn't mean they side with the Swartza. Isn't life funny?"

Nathanial shook his head but smirked up at

Bunny. He loved talking to her. It felt like she had all the answers. His stomach twisted as he dared himself to ask the next question. "Do you know anything about the blood curse?"

"That's an interesting question," she said, and chewed a little on the inside of her cheek. "Didn't you say Seizette stopped the one that was affecting Aliya? I think only the sprite that injects the blood curse can remove it. What's buggin' ya about it now?"

"I've been having nightmares that Aliya's curse will come back," he said honestly, and then added something else he'd been thinking. "And, you know, I almost had one put on me when I was in Swartza High. I tried to take the diamond trials, thinking if I became a Swartza I could call Sidian to rescue Aliya and me. Only after, I found out that if I'd succeeded then I would have been stricken with the blood curse for leaving. It got me thinking: we need to find a way to break that curse for sprites who don't want to remain slaves to Seizette." He was thinking of Jozy, too. What if she passed the trials and needed a way out? "I mean, there are so many Swartza out there. If any of them want to change, they're risking death to do it."

Bunny made a lot of noises as she wiggled in contemplation. "Good point," she finally said.

"Some wishes can break curses, which is why so many restrictions have been put on wish sprite abilities. Seizette is quick to quash any sprite whose power may match her own, but boy, oh boy, did she cross a line when she kidnapped Gem. Wait… that's it!"

"What?" Nathanial asked, reflecting Bunny's excitement.

"Gem! Not only does she have knowledge of wish sprite power, but she used to be a crystal grower! She's already told me that Seizette is using her diamonds to curse people. I bet Gem could figure out how to stop that ugly curse."

Nathanial jumped to his feet. "Let's go get her!"

THE CONTRAPTION

Bunny and Nathanial hurried outside to where they'd last seen Gem, but she was nowhere in sight. When they asked Pat about it, they were told she'd left with Aliya, so Nathanial and Bunny decided to try Aliya's room first. He knocked on the door and smiled when Aliya appeared though a little opened crack.

"Are you alone?" she whispered.

"I have Bunny with me. It's important we speak to Gem. Is she with you?" Nathanial asked, trying to peek inside.

"Yes. Come in." Aliya opened the door wide enough so that the two could enter before quickly shutting it again.

Gem sat cross-legged on the floor with the Truth Seer and all three wooden boxes open in front of her. Aliya's room was much like his own, small with domed walls of clay and a round glass window in the ceiling's center. A blue flower petal was currently swaying in the wind high above them, giving the room almost an underwater atmosphere. Only the essential furnishings of a bed, nightstand, and chair were provided, which explained why everyone gathered around the oval weaved rug that gave the room its lone splash of vibrant colors.

"Gem was telling me that she'd been hoping to be of more use stopping Seizette, but she hasn't been allowed in any of the Head Councilor meetings," Aliya explained. "I thought we could use her help with the Truth Seer that we borrowed from Amaranth."

"Oh, boy," Bunny said, rubbing her hands together. "Are we jumping in head first to the deep end? I love it!"

"Thanks for giving us a hand with this, Gem," Nathanial said. "Bunny was just talking about your old crystal growing abilities. I bet you can tap into the Truth Seer better than any of us."

Everyone joined Gem on the floor. She was still in her wooden armor from field practice, and her long, golden hair was slung over her shoulder in a braid.

"I'm definitely interested to see what all the fuss is about with this thing," Bunny said. "I heard that Amaranth had brought it to Sanctuary. But, like Gem said, the Head Councilor is keeping lots of his intel from those who aren't council members or trusted delegates. Understandable. The more people who know his plans, the more likely the Swartza will get wind of our next move."

"Exactly," Gem said. "Let's just hope the Head Councilor's inner circle is as trustworthy as he thinks they are. I don't blame Aliya for taking the Truth Seer from Amaranth quietly. I hope I can help you guys figure this thing out so you can return it quickly and without notice."

Nathanial nodded, and was thankful to have others on his side. "So, what have you figured out so far?"

"From what I can tell," Gem said, with shimmery lifted brows, "the diamonds in each of the three groups here serve a different purpose." She pointed from box to box as she explained. "This box is full of diamonds containing an individual sprite's complete set of raw memories. These are communication diamonds, most likely for sending direct messages. And these are memories that have been spliced together from multiple sprites. If you look here, you'll see this hidden door on the Truth Seer."

Gem slid open a small, square, metallic door near the base of the Truth Seer and pressed a button inside. The claws that held tight to the diamonds sprung open. She pressed it again and they closed.

"I believe that what you see from the Truth Seer depends on which diamonds are inside it."

"Have you watched any of them yet?" Nathanial asked.

"No," Gem said. "It's too dangerous. Seizette has to have access to each Truth Seer. She can both give and gather information, using them as conduits to any sprite that utilizes the device. Frankly, I think it's even dangerous for it to be within Sanctuary's walls."

"Amaranth is a spy, then!" Nathanial shouted.

Everyone hastily shushed him.

"We can't be sure of that," Gem said. "Amaranth could be using the device without knowing it's connected to Seizette. I would need to safely see what's in the communication crystals to be sure that she's knowingly betraying us."

"Gem's trying to build a crystal code that will block any transmissions that may activate when the Truth Seer is operating," Aliya said.

"This could take some time," Gem said.

"While we have you two here," Bunny started, and Nathanial's eyes widened in horror. Nathanial didn't want Bunny to ask about the curse in front of Aliya. He was sure it would worry her.

"No, that's okay, Bunny," Nathanial said. "They don't want to come try that thing with us."

"What thing?" Aliya asked with a lifted brow.

Bunny picked up what he was putting down and said, "New blood'n'grub soup at lunch. I thought you wanted to dare them to drink it with us?"

Nathanial kept shaking his head. "No, no, that's okay."

"Definitely not," Aliya said.

"I would, but I want to work on this. It'll take hours at the least. You go ahead," Gem said apologetically.

"That's okay!" Bunny said, hopping up. "Best leave the expert to work her magic on that sparkly tube of madness. Let's go then, Nat-a-booty. Just you and me shall brave this wonder of soup-making!"

Nathanial followed Bunny and waved goodbye to Aliya, saying, "See you later, then?"

"Sure," Aliya said, crinkling her nose.

Once they were a ways down the hall, Bunny said, simply, "Explain."

"Aliya's been through enough. If she knows we're trying to figure out a way to break the blood curse, it will be the only thing she'll be able to think about. It's already consumed so much of her life. I just don't want to worry her about it."

Bunny considered, then said, "But this *is* Aliya we are talking about?"

"Yes," Nathanial said, uncertainly.

"The girl that tempted you into a coup away from your sprite guardians to venture the unknown woods together. The girl who plotted a scheme to restructure sprite law? The girl who, instead of running back home to tell her family she's alive, is staying by your side while you try to encourage a rebellion?"

"What are you trying to say?" Nathanial asked.

"That Aliya is a tough girl. I bet she can handle it."

"I know she's tough." Nathanial pushed his curls back. "There's just too much going on without this weighing on her, too."

Bunny sighed. "Go with what your gut tells you, but I promise you it feels so much better when there aren't secrets between yourself and those you care about."

Nathanial pursed his lips. He knew her words were true: every secret felt like a knot in his gut. But the pain of it only worsened when he imagined the look on Aliya's face if he told her he was afraid the curse was going to return.

"Okay, maybe. Eventually," he said. "But for now, let's just hope that Gem can figure it out; see if she has any ideas on how to stop the blood curse. And then we can tell Aliya about it, if there's good news."

Bunny shrugged a shoulder and hooked his elbow into hers to continue their way towards food. Once there, Bunny declared that she was taking some biscuits and drink back to Gem and Aliya. Unfortunately, Nathanial knew he had lessons with Boss and Phlegm shortly after, and decided to stay behind and eat his assortment of nut pies in miserable solitude.

All of a sudden, Spassel slid into the booth next to him.

"Hey, buddy!" Spassel said, patting him on the back.

"Hey, Spassel. How's it going?"

"Good! I finally got the high jump without tripping up the landing. I might try the double jump tomorrow."

"That's good," Nathanial said with a small smile.

"Oh, look!" Spassel said, and Nathanial looked. The Head Councilor passed by with a group of delegates. "Wow! What I wouldn't do to talk to him alone for five minutes. He has so much on his plate right now. I bet he hasn't dealt with politics this complex since he passed that incentive law for pro-factory businesses. He really took some heat for that one."

"And you're still interested in being Head

Councilor one day?"

"Oh, you bet I am." Spassel nodded enthusiastically. "The more complicated, the better. I love problem solving."

"Not me. I can't wait for all this to be over so I can stop worrying every second of every day."

"But that's exactly the problem with having sprites in power that are against sprites like you and me. We'll always have to worry every second of every day if we don't have good representation to speak up for us." Spassel sighed. "You know, I used to think this Head Councilor wasn't strong enough to stand up for us, but he should at least have been allowed his full ten years of service. Kicking him out now after only seven years is a kick in the gut to any sprite who'd been given hope by the changes he was making.

"I just wished he'd been more open about what was happening with you, you know. If he hadn't've hid you being at Hyperion, he may have had a chance. Seizette wouldn't have been able to take you, and the public wouldn't be so distrusting of him now."

Right then, Mila slid onto the bench opposite Nathanial. "You've been mysteriously absent of late," she said, crunching on a cherry slice the size of her face.

"You're one to talk after what you pulled yesterday," Nathanial said.

"I got some more people interested in the debate," she said with a smirk. "We just might need an auditorium."

Nathanial froze. "Look," he said seriously, "I don't think it's such a good idea to be telling everyone about our debate. I may have some sensitive materials to use, and I can't do that if I think there might be a spy in the crowd."

Mila's expression fell. "Are you serious?"

Nathanial nodded insistently.

"Okay," Mila said, frowning and making eye contact with Spassel. "We won't tell anyone else."

"Thank you," Nathanial said. "Look, I better go." Spassel slid out to let Nathanial pass. "I want to call my mom before my private lessons. She hasn't been feeling too good lately. See you guys later."

Having the equivalent of FaceTime with his mom was always a bit of an ordeal, but Nathanial was willing to do the work for a couple of reasons. One, it was always good to see his mom rather than just hear her voice. And two, he knew he was going to have to get better at looking human for when he returned home for the summer.

He had asked Boss to teach him how to put a trick on the eye, like the one he'd seen Boss do to become a human-looking pirate once, but Boss explained that the sort of mental fortitude required for that trick would only come with age, practice, and patience. The last thing, Boss jested, Nathanial might never have.

Once in his room, Nathanial went straight over to his mirror. It helped him to know when he was successfully shifting his vibrations with visual confirmation. He licked his lips and concentrated on squishing down his pointed ear tips. Sometimes, if he was just too tired, he'd accomplish this using the ear cuffs Boss gave him, but he at least wanted to give it a go since the cuffs could easily slip off. Amazingly, his ears shifted to a nice round edge without too much strain.

Nathanial then reached for the melanin in his skin and stretched it over the golden hues that outlined his eyes like he was a part of a strange rock band. He'd long since told his mom the bits of orange and blue in his hair were a style he'd picked up from his new friends, because his hair was the first thing to change once at Sanctuary and he didn't yet know how to get rid of the colors.

Now that he looked passably human, he picked up his tablet and hit the VV symbol that stood for Visual Vibration. He sat on his bed and waited for his mother to answer.

"Hello?" his mother said, her pale oval face appearing on the screen.

"Mom!" Nathanial cried, joyful that she'd answered. Then he took notice of the dark circles around her eyes. "How are you feeling?"

"Oh, I don't feel as bad as I look," she said with a small smile, and brushed back the loose strands of brown hair that had escaped her ponytail. "Your old sterile room is coming in useful for me."

"Mom, you're not locking yourself in there, are you? That's no fun."

"No, no, darling. I go to the kitchen for mealtimes, but I just feel better when I'm in there. I'm one of the lucky ones, really. The hospitals are crazy crowded right now, and I still have such a good relationship with your old doctor, Doctor Ferguson, that he's giving me the care I need from home. I still work from my computer, too, so, I'm doing fine. I hear they'll have a vaccine within the year, and most people get better on their own.

"I'm just glad you aren't seeing any of this illness where you are. Your school sent me an email with all the precautions they're taking to keep you safe. You were sick for so much of your life, I think you've earned your health for the rest of it." She smiled sweetly, and looked to be teetering on telling him something more. "In fact, I've been getting a lot of calls about you from people I haven't heard from in a long time. With everyone in isolation, they're getting to experience for the first time what you went through for years. Just shows how hard it is for people to empathize unless they've gone through it themselves. It's like what Jane Goodall said about apathy being the greatest danger to our future."

She sighed before adding, "Even your father called."

Nathanial's heart tripped over a beat. His mother didn't like talking about his father. He'd left when Nathanial was just a baby; didn't want the shackles of a sick kid holding him back. Nathanial's only means of connection with his dad were the birthday gifts he received every year, and they were often things he didn't have much use for, like sports gear.

"Oh, yeah?" Nathanial managed to say. "What did he want?"

"To apologize," his mom said, obviously still processing it herself. "He was one of the first people who tested positive. He's been in quarantine for months. He says he doesn't know how you did it."

"You told him I did it with your help, right? And no thanks to him?"

His mom glanced away, her eyes glassy. "I didn't

say much of anything, really." She began to cough.

Nathanial saw two sprites on his mom's collarbone. They were tickling her throat, trying to produce the mucus they would then turn into sprite products. His mom covered her mouth with a handkerchief as she tried to catch her breath.

Nathanial's eyes narrowed at the sprites' callous actions. "Mom, let me give you some advice from an old pro: go take a long, hot bath. That's what I used to do when the coughing got too bad to handle. It helps. Do it twice a day, even."

He saw his idea had the desired effect, annoying the sprites. They stopped tickling his mom's throat and instead shook their fists at Nathanial. Nathanial knew it would be very difficult for them to keep working on his mom in the bath, and it would force them to leave her alone. At least for a while.

"Oh, a bath does sound wonderful right now," his mom agreed.

"Good," Nathanial said. "Hang in there. It'll get better soon, I promise."

"Thank you, baby. I love you so much."

"I love you, too, Mom."

The screen went black and Nathanial collapsed backward on his bed. He let go of the vibrations that held back his true form and shook off the chill that ran down his spine as a result. The entire world was looking more and more like the cage he'd lived in as an abused sprite factory. He needed to know this trend was not going to continue. And for that to happen, Seizette had to lose the vote to be the next Head Councilor.

He was determined to make it so.

LESSON LEARNED

Meeting with Boss and Phlegm always had a way of redirecting Nathanial's focus, which was why he was looking forward to seeing them back out on the field.

Phlegm had taught a class on vibrations back at Hyperion and, though he didn't look like much with his seaweed-colored greased-back hair and mucus-colored skin tones, Phlegm could tap quicker than you could spit. He kept to his routine of teaching Nathanial the most efficient ways of catching vibrations, and Nathanial was grateful.

Since the loss of his tap-aid necklace, Nathanial had needed to re-learn how to find vibrations without the easy plug-in. This was extremely difficult at first. He'd even begged Mila for another tap-aid that first week at Sanctuary. But she said he was suffering from power withdrawals, and it would be healthier for him to learn the right way. It did end up being better for him, especially since his battle blade already gave him an edge as it was.

Boss still helped Nathanial learn the dance of swordplay, but now he added the technique for wings. Teaching him wing control, camouflage, and maintenance was no easy task, but Nathanial's confidence had been piqued during the last artifact game, so it was a real blow to see that mark on his foot right at the end. After all his struggle to push past the pain of his mangled wings, he'd finally gotten through a scrimmage without even a twinge. Why did Boss always have to look so smug when Nathanial failed? On top of it all, Boss was withholding some secret wing maneuver as a prize if he were to win the game, and then made it impossible for him to win. He told himself Boss was just trying to instill the virtue of patience into him, but it was difficult to keep his temper about it sometimes.

"What do you guys have in store for me today?" Nathanial asked the pair, who were lounging on rocks by the tree line just beyond the stretch of Sanctuary's apartments.

"Boss an' I've just been havin' a lil chat about what to do about that raven of yours," Phlegm said, hands firmly planted behind his greasy head and legs stretched out in front of him—true to his Brooklyn demeanor.

"Boss already said Sidian could have another

chance," Nathanial said defiantly.

"Yeah, he's got his chance. But how's he going to prove himself, we was wonderin'?" Phlegm asked.

Nathanial looked from one to the other uncertainly.

Boss cleared his throat. "The problem is, I think he's not had enough time with you. We keep you so busy, it's really not fair to him."

Nathanial brightened. Was he going to get some free time with Sidian?

"He hasn't really had time to adjust, or had anyone to guide him. Sidian most likely spent his days training with other ravens before he went rogue. And lately, he just hasn't had any outlets," Boss continued, standing up from his rock and dusting off his coattails (which were actually the base of his wings). "He probably just got overexcited yesterday in the games."

"Exactly," Nathanial said in relief.

"So we've got some outlets planned for him." Phlegm picked back up. "Some locals have agreed to help us out here."

Phlegm got to his feet and yelled up into the vastness of the pine trees. "Come on down!"

Five gigantic bald eagles shrieked as they appeared as cuts against the blue sky and circled their way down, landing before them.

"Meet the Bald Battalion!" Phlegm said, grinning, and stood proudly next to one of their great talons. "Even if one of them's a lady and ain't got the white-feathered bald look about her head."

Nathanial gulped and craned his neck up at the colossal troop, then stood when he realized he'd instinctively crouched for cover. "How are they supposed to help?"

"We figure Sidian ain't used to birds bigger than him. They can give him a feel for what it's like, you know, to see where the smaller kind are coming from," said Phlegm.

"You want to intimidate him?" Nathanial lifted a brow. "That's a little mean-spirited, don't you think?"

"It will be good for him," Boss insisted.

"What exactly is the plan?" Nathanial rubbed his neck uncomfortably.

"We're going to have a little game of keep-away. The eagles will form a circle in the sky while you and Sidian fly in the middle. The eagles will throw a ball back and forth while you try to intercept." Phlegm clapped his hands together, a glint in his eye. "Why don't you give Sidian a call?"

Nathanial looked back and forth between Boss and Phlegm, then again to all of the gigantic eagles that were out to teach Sidian a lesson the old-fashioned way. "Can I at least talk to Sidian alone first?"

"Sure," Boss said.

Nathanial sighed and walked out into the middle of the low-cut grass of their training field before cupping his hands and calling, "Sidian!"

Only seconds went by before black wings glided to him from the nearby woods. Nathanial knew instinctively that Sidian was always just a call away. It made him both comforted and sad. Sidian had left all he'd known to join him at Sanctuary. The loneliness was undeniable, but the belief in what he was doing kept him standing by eternally, waiting for Nathanial's call.

"Hey, Sid. How are you?" The bird greeted him by way of a beak nipping at his curls.

Sidian gave a few clicks and a short caw.

Nathanial listened intently, then said, "I know. The thing is, they shouldn't have had to tell us it was against the rules."

Sidian scraped at the grass in front of him and cawed.

"You know things are different here. It takes some getting used to, having come from a place where rough games are the norm. But you said yourself they're crazy. You almost got electrocuted just for trying to get my attention through a window at Swartza High!"

Sidian cawed again.

"Look," Nathanial sighed. "Boss and Phlegm were kinda thinking along those lines. You know, that you're used to tough games and you need more of a… challenge."

Sidian perked up.

"They've got a game in mind for you… as an outlet for some of your… energy." Nathanial put it as nicely as possible.

Sidian jumped from foot to foot, cawing happily.

"Alright." Nathanial jumped up onto Sidian's neck. "It'd also be a good idea for us to work on our communication skills. No more taking me over without permission." Sidian nodded and Nathanial said, "Then let's do this."

They took to the air. Nathanial dug his hands into the wick of Sidian's neck feathers and felt the vibrations surging. Sidian was excited—or, he was, until the eagles began to circle.

Sidian clicked his beak back toward Nathanial.

"We're playing keep-away," Nathanial explained. "They're just going to toss a ball around, and we're going to try to catch it."

Nathanial's sweaty palms fiddled nervously. The dark brown female eagle had the ball. Sidian rushed her, and she threw it overhead to one of the boys. Nathanial felt the surge of surprise from Sidian upon closer proximity to the female.

Sidian cawed loudly as he swooped around and hovered back in the center. He made more clicking sounds.

"I know these guys are big, but remember yesterday? The advantage of the blue jay was that she was small and maneuverable."

Sidian cawed.

"No, Sidian, that's my point about having a different way of thinking. You don't turn an advantage like someone being smaller and quicker than you into *their* disadvantage by slamming them into the ground. These guys will show you how to handle the size difference the right way." *I hope*, he added in his mind.

Sidian tried to get into the zone of being a small, quick bird, but each time he'd swoop close to the roaring, beating, gusting wings of the eagles, he'd quickly chicken out and fly back to the center.

"I've got an idea," Nathanial said in low tones. "Size isn't really our advantage here, it's that we have each other. Remember how it was like I was an extension of you yesterday?"

Sidian cawed his agreement.

"Well, I need you to be an extension of me now. You'll have to let me be in control this time. Think you can do that?"

Sidian didn't respond for a moment. Nathanial felt a little bit of what was going on in Sidian's head: the raven had previously only ever been controlled by the Swartza. When they first met, he flew Nathanial on the orders of the Swartza. Since he'd rebelled, he'd wanted to be Nathanial's companion, but he never really saw himself having to take orders ever again.

"I'm not giving you an order," Nathanial said. "I'm asking you to trust me. I'm asking for permission."

Sidian nodded, and his tense vibrations began to loosen like changing strings on a violin. His quick heartbeat synced to the rhythm of Nathanial's drum, and the colorful sparks of red that represented Sidian merged with Nathanial's blue, flashing into purple swirls within Nathanial's unfocused eyes. Nathanial felt his extremities tingle and stretch out into expansive flapping wings. He was one with Sidian.

Nathanial took a gasping breath, his eyes dilated, and his vision tunneled before whipping back into an extreme wide-angle view of the world. He tried to flap the heavy wings, but this way of flying was alien to him, and he tumbled Sidian's body on a crash course to the ground.

Quickly, he adjusted the urge to flap the wings on his own back and shifted that strength into the wings of Sidian. Nathanial caught their tumbling bodies and pulled them back into the air. He had complete control over the two bodies. He'd never experienced such a thing before. Sidian had completely given himself over. He'd heard of an out of body experience before, but this had to be something else.

"Okay," he said, and the words came out of his sprite mouth and as a caw from Sidian's beak simultaneously.

Nathanial flew back into the center of the eagles, who had paused uncertainly.

"Bring it on," Nathanial said, and cawed.

The eagle with the ball in his claw looked around at his fellow Bald Battalion members and twisted his head with a shriek. He passed the ball to the eagle on his right.

Nathanial held his central position. The Battalion kept tossing it around, just out of reach. Nathanial knew he had to goad them into tossing it overhead. He flew quickly toward the possessor, but the ball went up high, too high to catch with Sidian's claw.

Nathanial angled Sidian sideways and ran up his left wing. He spread his shimmering shield into his beautiful sprite wings and jumped off. He flew up, caught the ball, and then brought Sidian underneath him to land victoriously on his back.

"Whoop!" Phlegm called loudly from underneath the circle. "Now that's vibrations wrangling!"

Nathanial let the raven's sensations rush out of his body to return to Sidian's control. He looked at the ball in his hand and shouted, "I can't believe we just did that! Can you believe it, Sid?"

Sidian did a victory flip in the air and cawed loudly. They and the Battalion landed in front of a cheering Boss and Phlegm. Nathanial jumped down, smiling, and patted Sidian's side.

Phlegm slapped Nathanial on the back. "Taught him everything he knows!"

"That was pretty impressive," Boss agreed. "Sidian deserves praise for letting you guide him like that. A very brave thing you both did up there."

Sidian nodded and clicked.

"Aw, thanks, buddy," Nathanial said, and received a nuzzle from Sidian. "He says I'm fun."

The eagles shrieked their congratulations and took back to the skies.

"That was crazy. I felt like a raven and a sprite all at the same time. Did you feel that, Sid?"

Sidian shook his feathers out and clicked.

"Oh, I know the tingling is weird. I felt that way when you had me yesterday, but this time seemed more fluid, you know? It's like I could move every part of you."

Phlegm looked to Boss and said, "I don't think I've ever heard it put like that before."

"No," Boss said, "not like that."

"What do you mean?" Nathanial shrugged. "I've seen Phlegm harness a dozen different animal vibrations."

"I can suggest a squirrel go left or right, but I don't move the feet myself, for crying out loud!" Phlegm was flabbergasted. "And the way you were able to keep such a strong connection when you jumped off him to catch that ball." Phlegm whistled. "That was somethin' else."

Nathanial licked his lips and looked up at Sidian, who suddenly cocked his head toward the trees, cawed, and took flight.

"He heard some bugs," Nathanial explained.

"You know," Boss said, watching Sidian disappear into the brush, "I think it's very special that he opens up to you like that. He doesn't let anyone else hear his thoughts. Not even Phlegm, who could have gone into animal whispering if not for his factory promotions."

"Shush it." Phlegm brushed the compliment

away.

"Well, he's the only one I can hear," Nathanial commented. "I don't know how Phlegm does it."

"If you two don't stop it I'll put both of you in charge of carrying this big head you're inflating on my shoulders. Now, let's go get dinner. I heard Pat saying there's going to be pineapple sculptures tonight. Should be *pretty tasty*. Get it? Pretty, tasty?"

"We get it, Phlegm," Boss said, rolling his eyes.

They all headed back to Sanctuary Hill.

A CRYSTAL-CLEAR MESSAGE

All the sprites of Sanctuary were ogling the dining area when Nathanial entered. "Pretty" had been an understatement for the pineapple sculptures. Each one of the towering centerpieces was uniquely carved and colored. They were shaped like fountains, floral bouquets, animals, and insects, just to name the few Nathanial could see.

When he reached his favorite nook table, the detailed barn owl sculpture delighted him. The chest was colored green, the heart-shaped face white, and its segregated feathers streamed multiple shades of speckled orange and yellow down its back. The pineapple husk still remained on its circular base, which took up most of the tabletop. Little triton forks protruded around the owl's claws.

"Isn't this amazing?" Aliya said, coming up beside Nathanial. "I feel like we should be wearing formal clothes or something. What do you think the occasion is?"

"Not sure," Nathanial said, fighting the urge to pick a feather and pop it into his mouth.

Mila came right up and pulled the beak off. "Hey, guys!" she said with a crunch, and slid into the curved booth.

Nathanial and Aliya exchanged disbelieving expressions that turned into laughter. They scooched into the booth opposite Mila.

"Whoa!" Spassel exclaimed, joining the group. "Isn't this the most nectarest thing you've ever seen?"

"Yeah, I won't have to look at your face for at least the first half of dinner," Mila jested.

Once all the sprites had settled into their tables, the antler-crowned Head Councilor stood, and everyone respectfully fell quiet. When he spoke, his voice resonated perfectly along the acoustic walls so everyone could hear, no matter their distance.

"I would like to call recognition to our wonderful volunteers who created this artful presentation. They wished to express their thanks to our honored delegates who have been in our company these past two weeks."

The room applauded toward the volunteers who outlined the walls.

"This is the last night the delegates are joining us, and we wish to send them off with a good taste in their mouths."

The room giggled, but Nathanial paused. If the delegates were leaving, then he wouldn't have to worry about Amaranth finding out he had her Truth Seer at the debate. But that also meant he wouldn't have a chance to return it to her. He squirmed in unease.

"I would also like to take this opportunity to convey how proud I have been to serve as Head Councilor. I must admit, I showed favor to the sprites I now see before me in this Sanctuary, progressive sprites who have been struggling to make a difference. You made factory friendly products to demonstrate success without sacrificing morals. You upheld the schools that taught us we could be anything we wanted to be, no matter our blood traits. The ideals we share may seem defeated as we gather under this hill, but I assure you now, that is not so. I have been working tirelessly to gather proof that your factories did not fail, and indeed, I am delighted to reveal that not only do I have that proof, but I have records reporting that your profits are higher than those of Thatcherville in its prime."

The room erupted in applause and Nathanial felt his cheeks turn red at the sound of his old citified name.

The Head Councilor smiled and waved for calm. "I will be leaving with the delegates to present this evidence to the rest of the council before the vote for a new Head Councilor. This should clear my reputation, re-instate my position, and give me the credibility I need to break up Big Lyso once and for all."

Everyone cheered again, and many stood at their tables.

Nathanial looked, amazed, at his friends. Mila had a look of triumph on her face, wiped her hands as if they'd been covered in crumbs, and said, "In the bag."

"Bon appetit!" the Head Councilor said in a raised voice, and sat down.

The entire room kept up the happy buzz throughout the food courses, giving Nathanial a twinge of guilt at his skepticism. He didn't want to ruin anybody's good time, so he kept his negative thoughts to himself—about the possible damage a Sanctuary spy could do from a position so close to the Head Councilor and his exonerating evidence.

Once Mila and Spassel departed boisterously, Nathanial asked Aliya if he could walk her to her dorm. She invited him in once there.

"Any luck with the Truth Seer?" he asked as she closed the door.

"Gem identified the transmitter and pulled it off the device," Aliya said, taking up a sock from her side table drawer and pouring a small circular diamond from it. "It was in the top. She says anyone who's asked it a question has had some of their memories transmitted directly to what she's calling Seizette's diamond hive." She put it back in the sock, threw it in the drawer, and slammed it shut. "I don't like it in the open. I think it's trying to read my mind."

Nathanial nodded. "Understandable. So this diamond hive is at Swartza High?"

"Yeah. It's how she knows who's loyal, who's on the fence, and who she needs to get rid of. She's been growing her sprite databank for a long time, using that school as an extra brain of sorts. She's probably been preparing for this new device the whole time, making room for the new flood of memories. There's even a receiver on it." Aliya showed him a similar diamond on the bottom of the Truth Seer. "Seizette can send any message, anytime. She's been throwing propaganda into the cities non-stop. If you wait a bit, you'll probably see one. They happen almost every hour."

"Did you ask it anything about sprites that fail Swartza High?"

"Yeah. It's what I figured and feared. She has

parents believing that their kids are only sent back to class for further studies when they fail the diamond trials. They have no idea that they're being imprisoned in the diamond for reconditioning."

"You would think they would know from going through it themselves."

"That's what I said to Gem, but she said a part of the reconditioning makes them forget they were reconditioned! But we know that—at least within the halls of Swartza High—there's some knowledge of what's going on while it's happening. Remember how the kids there threatened that we would be reconditioned if we didn't follow the rules?"

"Yeah, wow. That's crazy." Nathanial sat with that insanity for a moment, then asked, "What about those communication crystals? Any luck seeing what's on them?"

"No," Aliya said with a sigh. "They're locked."

"Like with a password?"

"Gem says a key."

Nathanial pondered. Aliya had stolen a key from Seizette's office in order to break him out of the diamond at Swartza High. "Do you still have that key you stole? The sparkly glove we used in the diamond."

Aliya looked puzzled, then lit up like a bulb. "Nathanial! You're brilliant!" She ran and pulled the diamond-encrusted glove from a drawer. "I forgot that I even had this." Aliya slipped it on and took a communication diamond from the maple box on the floor.

"Hey, wasn't there a third box?" Nathanial said, only spotting the two.

"Gem took the diamonds with the spliced memories in them. She wants to see what they look like without Codfear Brack's tainted messages all over them."

Nathanial nodded, then he and Aliya concentrated on the diamond in her palm. They stared at it for several long moments.

"Maybe you're supposed to say something," Nathanial guessed, but then he jumped back. The diamond glowed, and a gut-twisting sound accompanied it.

"Hello, Aliya and Nathanial." Seizette's sultry voice spoke from the sparkling crystal. They looked at each other, horrified. "Thanks to the time you spent in my diamond, I have the ability to predict your behaviors. You stole my captain's key from my desk, and only that key will activate this message. I'm sure you'll be disappointed that the key will not allow you to access any other information you may be looking for. If it makes you feel any better, I can assure you that nothing you may have learned otherwise would have told you anything more than what I am about to tell you now.

"The fight is over. I have won. Soon I will be Head Councilor, and on that day my army will raid Sanctuary and escort everyone back into the workplaces that suit their blood abilities. Anyone who refuses will be brought to me for reconditioning, or they can die trying to escape. I give you this chance to come back to me before my army arrives. I will be lenient. Refuse and suffer a decade in the diamond with the rest."

The diamond went dark, and the surrounding silence deafened them.

"If that isn't proof we're in trouble then I don't know what is," Nathanial said.

Just then, the Truth Seer awoke, spreading its arms and projecting its light so that the room transformed. It was as though Nathanial and Aliya hung like a cloud over an ash-coated mountain.

"This is one of her public announcements," Aliya explained.

The perky woman's voice that spoke to them from the device was now unfamiliar. "Here at beautiful Mount Lassen, where the Crossing Treaty was forged, is where leaders from all over the world will gather to cast their votes for our new

Head Councilor. But before that, this Friday, it will be the stage where our candidates will have a final opportunity to speak out on why they should be chosen. Even at this very moment, some of the most prestigious sprites in our history are filling these historical halls."

The imagery of the mountain filled their vision as if the memory being cast came from a sprite that was in quick flight down, toward, and into the massive volcano. At least a hundred sprites dressed in high fashion were filing into a decorative cavernous mouth at the peak. "Everyone is on porcupine quills to find out who the new Head Councilor will be. Ever since the disgrace of our last Head Councilor, sprites everywhere have turned their favor toward Lady Seizette, who promises a transparent government like we've never seen. Here is one reporter's memory from her travels on the campaign trail."

The room shifted, putting Nathanial and Aliya in the middle of a crowd full of sprites. All eyes were on a beautiful, diamond-studded Seizette in business attire, who stood tall and proud at a podium in the center of a coliseum.

"I hope you've come to understand why I made the tough decisions that I did when I was your queen," Seizette said to the crowd. "My only regret was not being open with you about them at the time. I knew it seemed cruel to put our abilities to full use on the factories, and I wanted to spare you that realization. But the alternative would have been for our kind to fall into ruin along with the rest of faery. Now, with my absence, you have seen that pro-factory business has crippled our economy."

A rush of nausea swept Nathanial. Thousands of sprites were in awe, drinking in her words like the nectar they craved.

"I've always believed in the power born inside each and every one of you, and if you put those blood abilities in their place, we will all rise to the greatest glory our society has ever seen. No more headquarters' cities crumbling into poverty. No more uncertainty as to where you belong. You can trust that your wellbeing is at the heart of everything I do. I am so proud that you all have made your voices heard and called for this election. I will, once again, pull us out of the dark, if you will allow me."

Applause roared through the wave of sprites as they rose to their feet. Nathanial was caught off guard by the elderly sprite next to him. She wore a tower of cotton balls on her head and they leaned precariously in his direction; she was clapping so hard they threatened to tumble off and onto him. He tried to push the fluff back into place but his hand passed right through it.

All the while Seizette continued her speech. "I want to bring you a sense of security with my election, as well. It's true that the downfall of the Head Councilor has stirred up a new rebellion from his supporters. After the vote of no confidence, the Head Councilor refused to turn over government power and kept it through force. If I had not lent my Swartza guards to aid in squashing this pathetic revolt, your will would not have been upheld. Give me full authority and watch as my fine Swartza Legion grinds this Fourth Rebellion to an immediate halt."

Seizette let the applause wash over her. Aliya and Nathanial glanced at each other, horror-struck, as Seizette continued.

"I have given every town a Truth Seer as part of my promise to be transparent, and I'm delighted to say that, for the first time ever, my device will allow for a live broadcast of the Head Councilor candidates' closing statements this Friday, and then the final elections the following week. I want everyone to be a part of this historic moment. Here's to a promise: that together we will start a new era of trust, prosperity, and security."

The applause was deafening, until it finally dissolved along with the images. Nathanial found he was suddenly alone with Aliya in her room.

"Do you think the Head Councilor's evidence will be enough to counter all that?" Aliya asked.

"I don't know." Nathanial licked his lips. "You don't think it's true about the Head Councilor, do you? Did he really refuse to step down?"

Aliya gaped at his question, then said, "Nathan, no. It's not true. Do you see how she just manipulated you into doubting the Head Councilor? It doesn't take much, does it?"

Nathanial pulled his fingers through his hair in frustration. "It's just hard to know what's real and what's fake. We can't be everywhere and see everything for ourselves all the time. We really need the person at the top to be trustworthy." He thought about how important it was to stop Seizette from holding such a seat of power, and how little time they had to do anything about it. "Those closing statements are the day after tomorrow."

"The same day as your debate with Mila."

"We should have the debate tomorrow." He decided on the spot. "I need to know if Mila has something more than what the Head Councilor told us tonight. This live broadcast event for the candidates' closing statements must be where the delegates and the Head Councilor are headed off to, to Mount Lassen. This is where they plan to show the evidence for the pro-factory profits. I need to know the Head Councilor has something more than what we've seen. Maybe Amaranth and Larix told Mila something that can really help, because, well, I'm just not so sure that sprites care about humans enough to let his evidence win him the support he needs."

"But Amaranth could be a spy," Aliya said, wringing her hands together. "Why else would she have diamonds with a hidden message directly from Seizette?"

"Maybe she didn't know the message was there?" Aliya looked skeptical. "Mila would be so pissed."

"No kidding. Amaranth is her goddess."

"Well, either way, we need to find out what Mila knows."

"Or what she thinks she knows."

They looked at each other, deep in thought, and then Nathanial stood up. "Guess there's nothing more we can do tonight," he said solemnly, and walked to the door. "Goodnight."

"Goodnight," Aliya said softly, frozen to the spot on the floor.

THE RETURNING ROAR

When Nathanial entered his room, he found a leaf the size of notebook paper flashing green on his pillow. When he reached down to pick it up, words began to form like worm bites, punching holes through the paper. He'd heard of this form of communication before: Boss mentioned it as the best way to contact him, since he didn't carry a tablet, but he'd never actually used it. He wondered why Boss would be using it now instead of just waiting to talk to him like usual. Unfortunately, it quickly became apparent that the message was not from Boss.

Nathanial Thatcher—There is only one way to break the blood curse upon Aliya. Meet me tonight. Come alone. Tell no one.

The words healed themselves with leafy particles and then reformed as a map. He recognized Sanctuary Hill and the field. There was an X in another clearing just north of the hill.

"X marks the spot," Nathanial whispered.

For a moment, he attempted to gather himself and think logically. Who had sent the message? Was it Seizette? Was she waiting for him in the woods? Not likely. She wouldn't risk herself like that. Most likely she was sending her captain after him again, Malik. She'd said in the Truth Seer message that she was giving Nathanial an opportunity to return before she raids Sanctuary. This must be it.

Now, what was he going to do about it? Should he go into the woods alone at night like he was told, or should he risk the consequences and ask someone for help?

No, he couldn't put Aliya's life on the line. There was still no answer as to how he could cure her curse without Seizette, and his fear that it had been reactivated now seemed to be confirmed. He put his long coat on over his wings and left with the map in hand.

Once out of Sanctuary, he followed the map as best he could. He'd circled the large hill toward the north and entered the woods, but after some time wandering without hitting a clearing, he felt like he was lost. He wondered if the battle blade could act as a guide but never really understood how the compass function worked.

The dark trees towered like skyscrapers over his spritely stature, and all the noises of the night were amplified in his pointed ears. An owl screeched, and he quickly pulled his battle blade from its ankle holster. He swished it into its sword form and waited for an attack that didn't come.

Nathanial slowly turned and attempted to retrace his steps. Suddenly, he noticed that every step he took had a mimicking step not far behind him. He stopped to listen. His mimic stopped. He started again, only for the mimic to follow suit. He quickened, and they quickened, until finally, he turned to ask, "Who's there?"

No one answered. The woods seemed to be too quiet now.

"Show yourself! I know you're there." Nathanial sounded braver than he felt.

"Bold words for a colorless sprite." The voice was deep and unfamiliar, speaking just behind the veil of darkness.

"Who are you?" Nathanial asked, pointing his sword in his stalker's direction. "How do you know me?"

"I know everything about you, Nathanial Thatcher. And I've come because you need my help." The owner of the voice remained in the dark.

"Are you the one who asked me out here? You want to help me save Aliya?"

"I do. I want to help both of you."

"Then do it," Nathanial said bluntly. "You can start by coming out of the shadows."

But maybe it would have been better for the voice to have stayed in the shadows. When the figure stepped out into the moonlight, he was twice as tall as Nathanial and armored to the teeth. An axe the size of Nathanial's whole body was gripped in one hand, a shield in the other. His black iron armor was imprinted with the Swartza symbol, keys crossing a sword.

Nathanial took it all in, gazing up to the jagged shards of the high helmet, and attempted to find the eyes that were consumed in the darkness of the iron slit. He'd seen this figure before, and he'd not expected to see it ever again.

"You're—" Nathanial's voice caught in his throat, and he cleared it to try again. "You're General Grantz. Seizette had you frozen in a block of diamond at Swartza High."

"*Queen* Seizette." The general emphasized the word with a snarl. "She kept my mind sharp with the memories of battle so that my strength would not diminish within these times of peace. I am grateful for it."

"I thought you were only supposed to be let out if there was a time of need."

"This is such a time."

Nathanial gulped. "I don't understand. Why do *you* want to talk to *me*?"

"You and I are much alike, and Queen Seizette wishes you to know it."

Nathanial did not respond. He looked the general up and down, not wishing to be anything like him—but he suspected he knew what the man meant. His eyes stopped on the axe. Its hilt was engraved with a spiraling battle, just like the sword in his own hand.

"We both have battle blades," Nathanial said. "So she did know I had one, all along."

General Grantz smiled, and a chill ran up Nathanial's spine. His four canine teeth had been filed into fangs.

"So what's the deal, then?" Nathanial asked, but looked away from the predatory grin. "What are you offering and what do you want in return?"

"I'm offering you these." He held out his palm, where two rings sat—the Swartza symbol, encrusted with diamonds, on each.

Nathanial licked his lips. "I've seen Sei—*Queen* Seizette give those to people who passed her trials. Why would I want them?"

"Do you recall this?" The general pulled a necklace out of his pocket. It was the one Mila had given him at Hyperion. Its heavy twisted metal amulet swung like a pendulum from the chain.

"It's a tap aid," Nathanial answered. "It helped me find vibrations and perform sprite tricks."

"Then you will understand how the rings work. It is a tremendous honor to receive them. Many Swartza owe their accomplishments to rings like these. They will amplify your talents to an extreme that you have never experienced before." General Grantz pocketed the rings and crushed the amulet into a ball. "This trinket does nothing in comparison to what you would feel with the ring." The general threw the crumpled metal into the dark woods. "And when you give the other to Aliya, her curse will be broken for good."

The words hung like a poison in the air. His heart pounded so loud in his ears it was hard to hear his own thoughts.

"As long as we stay in service to the Queen, you mean," Nathanial said, not needing the confirmation that never came. He knew it to be true. "What do I have to do?"

General Grantz flashed his frightening grin again. "Accept me as your mentor. You've already pointed out the battle blades. I think you know the meaning."

Nathanial sighed. "It means you're a changeling like me. A human turned sprite, and a sprite tapped the blade for you—probably when you were still human—putting some of their own abilities into the power of the blade. It might be why the blades are so powerful when we use them." Nathanial swallowed, but his mouth had gone dry. "Did Seizette tap your battle blade?"

The general's smile vanished. Nathanial didn't know what it meant. It hadn't seemed like an offensive question. General Grantz grunted and turned his back on Nathanial. "Follow me," he grumbled into the darkness.

Nathanial followed the giant strides of General Grantz until they came to a wide clearing surrounded by monstrous trees. A crate the size of his classroom in Sanctuary sat boldly in the center.

"What's this about?" Nathanial asked.

"A demonstration," the general said. "Stay where you are."

Nathanial took a couple of steps back. The general raised his axe with two hands and brought it crashing down onto the crate's lock, splintering it open.

Like it was Pandora's box from Greek myth, an explosion of horrible things swarmed into the air. Within the chaos, Nathanial saw transmogrified creatures from the Frankenstein displays of Swartza High come to life: porcupines with snake heads, wolf snarls from feline bodies, horned reptilian monsters, and flying abominations, all rising above the lot.

Nathanial instinctively took to his knee and lifted his sword, but the hoard's focus was only on the general. His axe swung left and right, separating the animals' anatomical mismatches into piles around him. Nathanial was horrifically astonished until his eyes rose to the sky, where dark wings formed an attack pattern. Poison dripped from the jaws of winged Komodo dragons, and they hissed at their target below.

All at once, their leathery wings tucked into scaly bodies and dove. Nathanial knew the general could not defend against the sheer density of the mass, and he found he wanted to look away. He couldn't.

At the last moment, as the swarm reached its target, the general took to one knee and lifted his shield above his head.

Nathanial wasn't sure what he was seeing. The dragons seemed to have hit the barrier... and then what? It looked like rain cascading onto an umbrella. Soon nothing was left of the attackers, except the dust that now circled the silent General Grantz.

The general lowered his shield and hooked the

axe onto his back. Nathanial didn't move. The general walked through the limp bodies of his first slain. He stopped in front of Nathanial and they stared at each other.

"A demonstration?" Nathanial finally said. "That was a slaughter."

The general did not respond.

"You know what I think?" Nathanial said in an intense whisper. " I think Seizette wanted you to scare me. To make me think I don't have a chance against you… or her."

"The demonstration," the general said slowly, "was to show you what you are capable of. No other sprite could do what I just did. No other sprite except you. And no other sprite could teach you these things, except for me."

Nathanial lifted an eyebrow. "How can you claim that?" Nathanial shifted his battle blade from its sword form to its staff form to its shield form, before finally letting it rest in its original knife form. "You didn't teach me that."

The general nodded and said, "Your current mentor, Boss, yes? He is at the limit of what he can teach you. Not only is he not the same as you—the way that I am—but he is also cursed, making his imagination weak and restricting his ability to communicate with you." The general took the axe from his back and clapped it to the shield in his hand. There was a bright spark and suddenly a battle blade knife, identical to Nathanial's, remained where the shield and axe had been.

"What happened to you?" Nathanial asked. "To make you like this?"

The general remained silent.

Nathanial feared the path that was being offered to him. He did not like seeing what he could become.

"Can I have some time to think about this?" Nathanial asked. He couldn't say no outright. Not only might it provoke the general to attack, but it might also damage Aliya's chance to fight her curse. Even worse, what if joining the Swartza was truly the only way to save Aliya? Would she join to save herself?

"To be expected," the general said with a single nod. "But I have to warn you— without the ring, Aliya's life is in greater danger than you realize."

"What do you mean?"

"Aliya has suffered crushed dreams, loss of family, imprisonment, and has even transformed into a thing she hates. The curse has woven its web and is now a ticking time bomb." Nathanial narrowed his eyes and clenched his fist. "But what you don't realize is there is also a trigger that could end her life before the clock winds down."

"Tell me," Nathanial demanded. "What trigger?"

The general turned to walk away. "Sidian still knows how to find us. When you are ready."

The sound of a bear's grunt came out of the darkness before the great beast itself did. It shook out its leathery wings while it met its master in the center of the clearing. The general jumped onto his beast and gave Nathanial one more long look before the bear roared and took flight. The pounding wind of their wake pushed deep into Nathanial's furious heart.

Somehow, Nathanial found his way back to Sanctuary. He could barely remember the walk, his mind was plagued with such horrible thoughts.

When he reached his bed, he sat and stared into the abyss for some time. He took up his pocket notebook and let his thoughts flow freely onto the pages, recording all that had just occurred. Then, after expelling all his doubts, worries, and despair, his fortitude came back to him.

The debate was tomorrow, and he needed to get Sanctuary on his side.

THE DEBATE

In class the next day, Nathanial found it hard to concentrate on anything Ms. Colette was teaching about warding off invasive ant colonies. Imaginings of an army led by General Grantz crunching down on Sanctuary repeated over and over in his head.

During breakfast, everyone had agreed to hold the debate out on the field later that day. That meant that when the axe of General Grantz wasn't busy swirling around in Nathanial's brain, he was frantically searching for articulate words that might convince the others to take action. He hoped that the Truth Seer would give him enough credibility. If he could show everyone Seizette's speech, they would see her lie about the pro-factory products causing a collapse in the economy. Then he would point out how she was blaming the Head Councilor for sparking a Fourth Rebellion, even though she had been preparing the Swartza for a rebellion way before the Head Councilor was forced to step down. Maybe, if he closed by reactivating the secret message that warned of her inevitable invasion, it would be enough to do the trick.

Class was soon dismissed, but Ms. Colette called Aliya's name to stay behind. Nathanial instinctively held back.

"It's okay, Nathan. You can hear this, too," Ms. Colette said, and waited for the rest of the class to exit.

Nathanial followed Aliya up to Ms. Colette's desk.

"There was a search of all quarters this morning for an important item that had gone missing from a delegate's chamber," Ms. Colette said softly.

Nathanial tried not to look automatically guilty, but he also knew it was probably pointless.

"They found what they were looking for in your room," she finished, looking to Aliya.

Aliya and Nathanial mirrored each other's stomach punched expressions.

"It was my fault," Nathanial said quickly. "I took it. I wanted it for a debate I'm having."

"It's okay, Nathanial," Aliya said. "I snuck us into Amaranth's room. I'm the one who should be punished."

"No," Nathanial said. "I'll take the blame. Please, Ms. Colette."

Ms. Colette held up her hand for silence.

"I'm glad you found someone who cares for you so much, sweet minette," Ms. Colette said to Aliya.

Aliya's eyes widened, and she looked to Ms. Colette in a new way.

"I am not going to punish either of you, though that is not what I told Amaranth. But she has left for the mountain with the Truth Seer, and there is no need to fear her retribution."

Nathanial was amazed at the kindness Ms. Colette exuded. She gazed upon Aliya much the same way as his own mother gazed upon him. He almost asked why she wasn't punishing them. But with his mother in his mind, he remembered her often saying: best not to look a gift horse in the mouth. He decided to appreciate his luck without explanation.

"Now, go have your debate," Ms. Colette said with a smile. "All of Sanctuary has been in a buzz about it—and good luck to you two. I'm always for taking action over doing nothing."

As Nathanial and Aliya walked away down the tubular hallway, Nathanial said, "Can you believe it? I mean, I'm glad we weren't punished, but we lost the Truth Seer."

"I believe it," she said frankly. "I have the worst luck. We just lost our best evidence."

Nathanial groaned. "Right."

"Actually, I wonder if they found the diamond in my sock drawer."

"The transmitter?" Nathanial asked.

"Yeah. But I'm not sure what good it could do."

Nathanial suddenly remembered his other piece of planned evidence. "What about the communication crystal that showed us that secret message? Do you think they took those, too?"

Aliya's eyes widened.

"Go check," Nathanial said, trying to reorganize his plan. "And let's dress for the occasion, put on our armor, and bring everything out onto the field. I have something in my room that might work in place of the Truth Seer. I'll meet you out there."

Shortly after, they met back out on the sun-soaked field, greeted by a whirling breeze that shifted the bordering flowers into a lulling dance. But it was not their hypnotic motion that made the scene a dizzying sight: Spassel and Mila stood in front of a couple hundred chattering sprites.

Nathanial froze. Spassel looked at him apologetically.

"Any luck with those communication crystals?" Nathanial squeaked to Aliya.

She shook her head. "Remember what I said about my luck," she explained.

They stood by a root that had been recently

raised out of the ground and formed into a rough stage for the debate. Bunny and Gem waited by its bumpy staircase.

"Hey," Nathanial said to them, feeling his mouth dry up like the Sahara.

"Hey!" Bunny said proudly.

"You okay?" Gem asked, glancing at his pale face.

"Yeah. Sure," Nathanial forced out.

Phlegm walked up and hit Nathanial on the back. "You just never quit, do ya?" He laughed. "Wish Boss was here to see this. He'd tear you a new one."

"Where is he?" Nathanial asked, surprised.

"He's escortin' the Head Councilor to Lassen. The old chief has a soft spot for our Mr. Blue," Phlegm said with a snort.

Mila and Spassel walked up to the podium on the stage. She turned around and waved for Nathanial to join them. The crowd cheered as he and Aliya went up the stairs. Nathanial's legs might as well have been back on the *Argosy*. He guzzled in the sweet air to steady himself.

Spassel pulled a two-toned coin from his pocket. "Blue or white?" he asked.

"Mila can go first," Nathanial said.

Mila laughed and said, "Fine with me."

Mila took to the twisted root podium, set her tablet on its branched surface, and waved at the cheering sprites. Her voice reverberated against curved elephant leaves that bowed around the corners of the crowd.

"Good afternoon, my fellows," she said, and Nathanial was amazed at how suddenly classy Mila looked, as if she'd taken a page out of Amaranth's stylebook. Her hair was pulled back out of her face and clipped up with purple cacti flowers. She wore a thick dark dress suit with large spike-y buttons down the front, and her high boots had high heels. She'd definitely dressed for the occasion. While he looked ready for battle, she looked ready to crush the debate.

"The topic of this debate is: do we, the residents of Sanctuary, need to take action against Lady Seizette's threat of taking over? Or can we trust the representatives we've gathered to make the stand for us? I say that we can trust our representatives, and here are the reasons why.

"First off, you all heard the Head Councilor's speech last night. He is on his way to present that evidence for us as I speak. Soon the world will know that pro-factory operations are our profitable future."

Applause took up with the remembrance of the

previous night's hopeful speech. When the roar subsided, Mila continued.

"Also, I had the privilege of speaking with two of the most respected delegates who joined us. One of them, Delegate Larix, is from South Africa, where the pro-factory mentality never took root after the Third Rebellion. He did not understand our position until his involvement here. His turn of opinion is proof that our representatives can help any sprite to understand our perspective."

"Then there is Amaranth, whom we all know was widely responsible for informing us of Lady Seizette's dreadful plans to enslave any who opposed her before the war. Amaranth thereby ensured our freedoms by outing this information. She has assured me and my impartial witness," she gestured to Spassel, who stood beside her, "that she and the majority of the delegates will be able to reappoint the Head Councilor once his name is cleared at tomorrow's event. Not only will he show everyone that his support of pro-factories was profitable, but that it is admirable as well."

Again, the crowd applauded. Nathanial pulled at his fingernails. He could see the confidence in their eyes, their hope in the truth that Mila spoke. How could he crush those optimistic faces down into his reality?

"In conclusion, everyone will soon be able to return to pro-factory jobs and self-enhancing goals without fear of the recently written laws or retaliation," Mila ramped up her voice for the speech's finale, "for they will be abolished by our trusted representatives once they are securely back in office with renewed support from spritekind," and she thrust her fist into the air.

Mila stepped down proudly, waving to the crowd that so obviously supported her with their cheers.

Nathanial felt faint. He hadn't written a prepared speech like Mila. He didn't have a nice suit. He didn't have the Truth Seer. He didn't have the communication diamond, and he didn't have supporters. Then, he felt something in his hand. Aliya had put the diamond glove and a sock into his palm.

"I did find these," she whispered. "Maybe worth a shot."

Nathanial took to the podium and stood in silence. A sea of skeptical eyes bore into him. What was he going to say? He'd read somewhere that public speaking was most people's number one fear, and with his voice stuck in his throat he began to agree.

He pulled out his pocket notebook and concentrated on his reasons for standing there. "No one wants to believe that our representatives are outmatched. We've been training for the worst-case scenario without actually believing it could happen. I'm glad, at least, that we are prepared.

"I was going to use the Truth Seer to show you how Seizette is still gaining sprite approval beyond these walls, but Amaranth has taken it. However, I do still have this."

He held up his pocket notebook. "It's everything I've been through. People wiser than me have said it's hard to empathize with something you haven't been through; that apathy is the greatest danger to our future. I'm hoping that you will be able to understand where I'm coming from if you read this."

Nathanial took the tablet out from a fold in his chest of armor and clicked the symbol that looked like the Egyptian Eye of Ra. The same symbol was in his notebook. He'd learned recently from Ms. Colette that you could upload or download information to and from devices that had this symbol. He wished he'd known that when he'd had the Crossing Treaty book in his possession. It would have been a lot easier to copy some of its vital notes.

He put one finger on the tablet's eye and one on the notebook's identical symbol. The tablet requested if the upload should commence to all local devices. Nathanial clicked *yes*.

"You should all be able to access my writings from your tablet now, but I'm not so naïve to think that most of you will read it." There was soft laughter, but a few sprites were actually pulling out their tablets. "Even where I'm from, reading isn't the first go-to source of information. So…" Nathanial said, and put on the diamond glove. "I'm going to try something a little risky here."

This got everyone's attention. A tense silence filtered through the crowd as Nathanial poured the transmitter diamond out of the sock and into his hand. "I don't know what this is going to do, but I'm told it's worth a shot."

He looked hopefully toward Aliya, who nodded anxiously.

Moments of a heavy nothing passed through the uncertain company of Sanctuary until a shattering, startling voice gripped the sprites in horror. "Nathanial Thatcher." Seizette's voice boomed out from his palm. "You have one of my transmitter diamonds. Let's see what new secrets you have to share with me."

A beam of light burst upwards from Nathanial's diamond-studded hand, creating a broken projection of images high in the air. Nathanial was re-experiencing his failure of the diamond trials. He felt the torturous electric jolts Seizette had used on him for reconditioning, and he uncontrollably shouted, "Lady Seizette, my Queen! How could I betray you? Forgive me! I'll do anything that you ask!"

Seizette's cold laugh echoed through the spectators, who gasped and backed away from the traitor in their midst. Nathanial fell to his knees and Aliya dropped to his side.

"Nathanial, let go!" she yelled at him. "Nathan, stop clenching your fist, she's trying to get in your head!"

But the distorted, out-of-order memories continued to beam up and confuse the audience, who struggled to make sense out of what they were seeing.

Aliya looked up at them and said, "Wait, Nathan. Maybe you can use this to your advantage. Don't let her control you. Block her out. You have to take control!"

Nathanial's eyes were still closed and he was still shaking, but Aliya persisted. His breathing had calmed at her words.

"Try to focus on what the communication crystal told us. Can you do that? Concentrate on Seizette's hidden message to us, her threat to us. Concentrate, Nathan!"

Nathanial let Aliya guide him past the punishments of Seizette in his mind. Her voice was stronger than that of Seizette. Her voice meant more to him than anything. He knew what Aliya was trying to tell him to do, and he concentrated on what he wanted to share with Sanctuary.

An image of Seizette addressing the crowds as he had seen through the Truth Seer solidified as a clear projection above him. He remembered her threat to him and heard the words blasting out for all to hear: "The fight is over. I have won. Soon I will be Head Councilor, and on that day my army will raid Sanctuary and escort everyone back into the workplaces that suit their blood abilities. Anyone who refuses will be brought to me for reconditioning, or they can die trying to escape."

Then, he pushed forth the gargantuan memory of General Grantz. The great winged bear roared and spread its wings in front of the horrified crowd. Screams accompanied the intimidating concept of their greatest enemy's return.

"You did it!" Aliya said, turning her attention back onto Nathanial. All of the projections above the stage had vanished. Nathanial twitched, his eyes sealed shut. "You can let go now." Aliya wrenched at Nathanial's clenched gloved palm, but it held firm. She put her hands on his shoulders, shook him, and screamed, "Let go!"

He opened his eyes and they locked with hers. Memories flooded directly from him and into her. "Aliya," he whispered. "I'm sorry."

They were sharing the moment Nathanial had been so tortured over. The moment Aliya's mother looked at her newborn daughter with unconditional love for the first and last time.

Aliya's eyes rolled back into her head and she passed out. The diamond fell from Nathanial's palm.

"Aliya?" Nathanial gasped, and rolled her over. She was limp in his arms. "Aliya!" he shouted again. No response.

Bunny and Gem rushed to their sides.

"What happened?" Bunny asked in horrified concern.

Gem picked the diamond off the floor. "It was this transmitter," she said, rolling it over in her palm. "It wasn't built to be used outside of the Truth Seer like that. Seizette tried to reach

Nathanial but he fought it, forced the thing to project what he wanted. When his powerful abilities combined with that glove, it amplified memory transmissions."

Nathanial frantically explained, "It's the curse. The blood curse. Seizette reactivated it. I felt it trigger when she experienced the love of her mother, but it was more than that even, it was her seeing how much I wanted to protect her from this, how much I…"

"Unconditional love," Gem said. "The blood curse ends the life of its victim if they find unconditional love. How cruel."

"Gem, can you break it? Can you stop the blood curse? You were a crystal sprite, a wish sprite. You fought against Seizette's power in the diamond. Is there anything…?"

Gem pulled back. "I don't know," she said, but then pursed her lips, took a breath, and leaned down toward Aliya and asked Nathanial, "Remember how you were able to help me navigate through the diamond?" Nathanial nodded and let Gem guide his hand onto Aliya's forehead. "You have the power to tap into many abilities. In that case, you boosted mine by tapping into Seizette's diamond ability. Maybe we can do that again." Gem closed her eyes. After excruciating moments of silence, she said, "There it is. It's almost to her heart…" Gem squeezed Nathanial's hand tight and he could see it then; the black barbed wire of a curse just inches from its stranglehold. "Ugh, I can't…" She burst out an exhale. "I slowed the curse, but I can't stop it."

Nathanial shook his head, tendrils of despair threatening to wrench out of his own heart.

"I need more time with Aliya," Gem added. "Maybe if I come at it from a different angle."

"We don't have time," Nathanial said, having seen the curse's claws longing for Aliya's end. "But you can come with us Gem."

"What? Where are you going?" Bunny asked, but Nathanial was on his feet and cupping his hands.

"Sidian!" he called, but the raven had sensed Nathanial's need and was already swooping down from the sky. Sidian scooped Nathanial, Aliya, and Gem into his beak.

Nathanial held tight to Aliya as Sidian dropped all three of them into the riding groove behind his neck. Gem sprawled out and screamed, her white-knuckled grip holding tight to black feathers as Sidian took them all up into the air.

"You know where I want to go, Sid?" Nathanial asked, and received a caw in reply.

"Where are we going?" Gem yelled over to Nathanial.

"To someone who can save her. But if you can figure out a cure before we get there, that would be best for us all."

To Mount Lassen

Gem had been searching Aliya's vibrations for over an hour, as they flew over increasingly rocky terrain.

"Anything?" Nathanial asked for the half-dozenth time.

"I think I've found it," Gem said.

"Really!" he exclaimed. "What did you find?"

"The source of the curse strain. It's diamonds, deep in her blood. The crystal gives me *some* insight… but Seizette is the only one who can manipulate this curse. Who is it that you think can help her?"

Nathanial knitted his brows. He didn't know how Gem would react to hearing they were headed into enemy territory.

Sidian gave out a caw and Nathanial turned his attention forward. "What is it, Sid?"

But no reply was necessary when he saw the sight before them. Like a dark cloud blowing onward above the tree line, a conspiracy of ravens cawed and clicked a hundred yards ahead. As they moved closer and into their midst, the ravens began to notice their new company with dismay.

Nathanial's feeling of unease intensified when angry caws shouted at them from each side. "Uh, Sidian, what's the plan here?"

The raven to their right looked particularly upset that they were not heeding any of his shrieks and rammed them. They screamed, and Nathanial's tight hold of Aliya proved not quite tight enough. Her limp body twisted away from his grip. He frantically pulled at her, knowing his own wings could not support them both if they tumbled. Gem reached over from behind Nathanial and helped push Aliya upright again.

"Sidian, get us out of here!" Nathanial yelled.

Sidian dived below the treetops. Their attacker took pursuit. As they raced along, Sidian used evasive maneuvers, but received several nips at his tail feathers nevertheless. Swerving around trees and under branches, Nathanial felt his grip strength being tested again: Aliya's weight had shifted edgewise. If he readjusted for a better grasp at the wrong moment, he would lose her.

"Sidian, I can't hold on much longer!" he shouted, his voice taut.

Changing tactics, Sidian lifted his body, slowed his speed, and dropped toward the ground. The flock passed over as Sidian continued his descent.

It was then that the cannonball dropped into Nathanial's stomach. They were coming down into the middle of a sprite army. It stretched beyond eyesight, along a winding dirt road. Between the battalions of soldiers were two giant centipedes, interlocked with chains, one behind the other, giving them the look of a train. Many colorful box carriages were strapped along their backs, and flanking them were a few dozen harnessed transmogrified beasts.

About fifty armed soldiers cleared a landing circle for Sidian to settle in, and looked more surprised than threatened by the incoming bird. None of them drew their swords, but their hands were upon their hilts just in case.

An importantly decorated sprite flew in to face them. On landing his wings folded perfectly into concealment amidst his dark uniform. His helmet plume was red, and high upon his head. From the center of his disturbed battalion, he asked, "What's your business, raven? Why have you brought us these sprites?"

Sidian cawed and, for the first time, Nathanial could not understand him. He could tell the officer did though.

Just then the raven who had nipped at Sidian

landed behind them and gave a few caws of his own. The officer looked between the two ravens, then flew to the centipede behind them.

"What's going on?" Nathanial asked Sidian. To his horror, there was no response.

Nathanial looked to the front centipede where the officer had flown and felt the world fall away as a beautifully adorned Seizette stepped out from the immaculate carriage atop its head. She smiled sparkles of red in his direction. Her heavy beaded dress would have trailed behind her as she moved toward the top step, but was ringed upon her middle finger instead. The troops lowered steps and parted a path for her that led to Nathanial's clearing. She didn't bother to walk it.

"Well hello, Nathanial," Seizette said with mild interest. "Seems you're trying to tie our deal at the end of your rope."

Nathanial couldn't speak. He'd expected to be brought to General Grantz for the rings, not to be dropped smack dab in front of the rings' source of power.

"I believe you were warned this would happen," Seizette continued coldly. "You should have come immediately. I'm far too busy to bother with you right now." She turned back to enter her carriage. "Put them with the rest. We don't stop again until we've arrived."

"No!" Nathanial called to the disappearing diamond-studded back. "Please, she's dying!"

But Seizette did not turn. A squad of troops flew up to them and forced them from Sidian's back. The other raven began to peck at Sidian's side and bullied him up into the air. Nathanial and Gem were thrown into a long carriage at the back of the trailing centipede. Nathanial turned and caught Aliya before she hit the floor hard, then he rushed to the closing door and shook, kicked, and banged against its sturdy lock. He felt the centipede beneath them wave its legs into motion.

Nathanial threw his fingers back into his wind-tossed hair. "What have I done now?"

Gem was too busy exploring their new surroundings to answer, running her fingers along the rough diamond walls. Nathanial tried to see down to the end of the seemingly infinite hallway, which waved and swayed with the movement of the centipede. The diamond cell most likely stretched the creatures' entire length.

"There are people in here," Gem said, and stopped at a particular protrusion.

Nathanial rushed by her side. "Boss!" he exclaimed. His mentor was pale, frozen in the wall. "Can you do anything?"

"Mmm," Gem contemplated. "Do you still have that diamond glove key?"

Nathanial snatched it from his pocket and handed it to her. "It has a lock on it, and Seizette knows I have it."

"I might be able to work with that," Gem said, twiddling with the fingers.

"You're like a hacker, aren't you?" Nathanial asked. "Bunny was right about Seizette making a big mistake when she messed with you."

"Seizette's made worse mistakes than me," Gem said softly, in concentration. "Here. I think I've reversed the poles of recognition it had locked on you. Instead of repelling you, it should be inviting. But that means you're the one who has to do this."

"Okay," Nathanial said, taking the glove back. "Do what?"

"Go get Boss," Gem said, and gestured toward the diamond.

"In the diamond?" Nathanial asked, surprised. "I can't just pull him out from here?"

"Not without sending him into shock. He'll be immersed in his own memories right now. More than likely they're tragic ones."

Nathanial remembered when he was trapped in the diamond; he had relived one of his cough attacks.

"So what do I do?" Nathanial asked uncomfortably. "Are you sure there's no way for you to do this? Or we could do it together, like when we saved Spassel?"

"I need to stay with Aliya. When I'm connected to her, I can almost keep the curse from moving at all. Now, when you find Boss, you'll need to remind him of who he is, who you are, and that he's just in a memory. You can talk him out. With the key, you'll see the doorway to the exit."

Nathanial licked his lips and took a fortifying breath. He pushed the gloved hand into the diamond, grabbed Boss by the wrist, and stepped into the wall.

At first, the sound was muted, and his vision was a white blur. This was surprising, because Nathanial had expected to see Boss right next to him. He'd grabbed hold of Boss's wrist with the exact intention of not having to search for him once inside the vast prison. This told Nathanial that he was seeing things from inside his mind, and not with his eyes.

Then there was the faint echo of a scream. Nathanial turned toward it.

"Boss?" he called out, but there was no reply.

The blur began to solidify. Colors took shape as patterned walls, carpeted floors, and crystalline ceilings. Two figures stood by a distant window, looking away from him.

"This land is ours, my darling," said a whisper, as if upon his own ear. It sent shivers down Nathanial's spine. "Isn't it glorious?" The woman brushed her hand through the man's dark blue hair.

Nathanial felt the room coalesce, and he suddenly stood beside the pair. His heart jumped to see Seizette looking at Boss the way a lover would. Boss did not look at her in kind. In fact, his look was of… nothing. It was so blank and so troubling that Nathanial didn't wait another moment to see where this strange memory was going.

"Boss," Nathanial said, weakly. He didn't know how the Seizette memory would take to his presence, but he didn't have time to linger.

When neither responded, Nathanial took hold of Boss's wrist the way he thought he had through the diamond wall. A barrage of images, feelings, and knowledge plunged into Nathanial's mind. He knew what was happening because it had happened before in the diamond. He was downloading memories—Boss's memories.

It was hard to understand it all; Boss had lived

what felt like several lifetimes. He could see him as an uncolored youth for only a moment, using sticks for swordplay with his father, whose skin sparkled like diamonds in the sunlight. When Boss began to bud with shimmering skin of his own, he confessed to his parents that he was trading his color in. That he would become a brave golden warrior. He was scolded throughout adolescence for this aspiration, until something new caught Boss's attention.

Nathanial witnessed a color change that was not yet gold. Boss became tan, with black hair and brown eyes; he shrank his ear points down and snuck out onto the cobbled streets of an old shipyard where the *Argosy* docked. There, he talked to a young lady with long blonde hair rippling out from beneath her bonnet. She told him stories, which she called fairy tales.

He went to her often, indulging her fascination with the stories she believed to be myth until, one day, he couldn't help but tell her who he really was—*what* he really was—and that she, too, was living a kind of fairy tale. She and her port town sat on the edge of two worlds. If she wanted, she could join him to explore even grander lands than she could even imagine. Would she join him?

The revelation did not have the effect that Boss

had hoped. The idea that she was living in a bubble of time separate from the real world frightened her. She ran away. But she couldn't have known that, once out of the bubble, there was no way for a human to find that port town.

Boss never saw her golden hair again.

Then there were visions of riots, chaos in the streets, and effigies of Queen Seizette burning in town centers. Boss became the golden hero he'd always wanted to be, but quickly realized that he preferred words to the sword. He would speak to the crowds about peaceful means to fight back. He led factory strikes and town meetings. But the bloody war came down upon them anyway.

The next memory had been hard for Nathanial to witness when he was in the Diamond Trials, but now, from within Boss's own memories, it was almost unbearable. Seizette put her hand on Boss and shook the very foundation of who he was. Everything he believed turned against him in his mind. He saw visions of those he'd led on strike screaming blame at him for their deaths on the battlefield. He saw humans taking advantage of the sprites and leaving them in ruin. He saw Seizette wiping the fields clean of blood and lifting him to his feet a new man.

"You were right, my Queen," Boss said,

monotone. "Please forgive me."

Nathanial slapped himself across the cheek, willing himself to break free of the flooding memories. He blinked and saw Boss standing like stone next to him, his wrist still in Nathanial's hand.

"Boss, come on, now." Nathanial pulled at him. "I know you've gotten through this before. How did you do that?"

The room spun like a tornado and landed in another day. Boss was both next to him, in his hand, and in the middle of the room, on his knees, pulling at his hair.

A yellow sprite girl in maid attire snuck into the door, quietly. She ran on tiptoe down to Boss's side.

"Conrad, please," she said into his ear. "You must get up. This is your only chance."

"Why do you call me that?" Boss asked the girl, not looking at her. "You are the only one who calls me that."

"Because," she whispered into his ear, "we knew each other once. It took me a long time to find you again. Only I fear I am too late."

Nathanial walked closer to the huddled couple and saw the familiar features of the youthful village girl who had once been human. Now, her hair was closer to the color of straw, and was cropped tight around her pointed ears.

Boss looked at her, unrecognizing and confused.

"Please, you must go. Now," she said, pulling him to his feet.

The girl escorted him out of the room. The Boss that remained watched them go. Nathanial jerked—Boss was awake!

"Boss, can you hear me?" Nathanial asked.

Boss blinked and slowly focused on Nathanial. "What are you doing here?"

"What am I doing here?" Nathanial repeated. "What does it look like I'm doing? I'm trying to rescue you!"

Boss stared, then the room shifted into towering woods. "Oh," he said, realizing. "We're in Seizette's diamond hell. This is the last thing I can remember happening before..."

Nathanial saw the Head Councilor surrounded by Swartza guards. Seizette approached the memory of Boss, who had clearly knocked down many troops. They were being picked up off the ground around him, but it was obvious he couldn't have persisted against their overwhelming numbers.

Seizette put her hand upon his cheek. "What a pleasant surprise. I thought you were dead until I saw young Nathanial's memory of you. How cute you've been trying to push past my curse all these years. I don't think you've managed it well. It shouldn't take long to finish your reconditioning, and when you revert back into the beautiful diamond skin you were born to, we can finally bathe in each others' brilliance as we were meant to."

The real Boss wiped the image of Seizette away. She dissipated like smoke. "I don't think so," Boss said, and turned to Nathanial. "So, you have a way out of here?"

Nathanial's head shrunk back into his shoulders. "That's it? You're okay? I thought it'd be a little harder. I thought I was going to have to remind you of who you were and… stuff."

"I've been through this charade before. All I needed was for you to get my attention. Now, I'm eager to get out of here, if you don't mind."

Nathanial shook his head and looked around. The woods were fading into a misty white nothingness. He'd hoped the exit Gem had mentioned would be obvious. He looked twice over every negative space before he saw a thin square outline.

"There," Nathanial said. "That must be it."

They jogged toward it and almost went through until Nathanial stopped. To his left was a series of square outlines that formed a hall down into the white. Faint screams echoed from the corridor.

"There are more people down there," Nathanial said.

"Of course there are. This is a vast prison. But we need to go."

Nathanial didn't move. He could just barely see someone behind the fog in the next room over. Something about him pulled Nathanial in.

"Nathanial, stop! What do you think you're doing?" Boss tried to hold Nathanial back, but Nathanial needed to see this. He pushed Boss out of the exit and moved into the next cell, alone.

BUMPASS HELL

Beyond the fog, a beautiful stone cottage cut from a boulder sat at the base of a skyscraper tree. A tall, tanned sprite man and a petal-pink woman with full lips and wavy cotton candy hair sat in one another's arms in the hollow of a scooped-out mushroom. The woman fed a sliced berry to the man, and they laughed.

Suddenly, they were surrounded. Swords pointed at them from uniformed sprites, and a captain landed before them.

"General Grantz and Lady Jessabelle." The captain spoke authoritatively. "You are under arrest for desertion of your posts in a time of critical need. General Grantz, you will be returned to your duty. Lady Jessabelle will be imprisoned until the general has adequately performed the wishes of our Queen."

The general jumped down from the mushroom, pulled his battle blade from his side—and then something went haywire in the memory. An explosion seemed to emanate outward from

General Grantz himself. All of the sprites were dead except for the general. The cottage lay in ruins. The scene jumped to General Grantz weeping over his dead love. Without warning, his red eyes locked onto Nathanial.

The monster that the general had become, wracked with this grief, flashed into terrifying reality before Nathanial's eyes. The winged bear suddenly appeared, roaring, and Nathanial stumbled back in shock. General Grantz spiraled his axe over his armored body and crashed it down on hordes of attacking sprites.

Nathanial screamed and jumped out of the diamonds' exit behind him. "Whoa!" Nathanial hopped in place from the spike of adrenaline, now safe in the company of Gem and Boss. "General Grantz is in there, and boy is he angry."

"Yes," Gem said softly. "Seizette keeps him in there when she's not using him."

"So his strength doesn't diminish." Nathanial repeated the words the general had spoken in the forest. "Yeah, I've heard. But it looks more like he's just torturing himself."

"I think there's more going on in the diamond than we've realized," Gem said. "It feels like she's put everyone from the Swartza High diamond into this mobile centipede train of hers. Why would she bother to do that?"

The centipede stopped, and Nathanial ran to the back door to gaze out the small window. A horrible rotten egg smell came in through the thorny bars. Night was falling outside on a landscape that looked plucked from Jupiter's moon Io, a volcanic satellite. Steam poured from yellow and white fractures scattered through the barren hills around them. Mudpots bubbled and plopped alongside sapphire blue pools of water.

"What is this place?" Nathanial asked, curling his nose.

Boss peeked over his shoulder. "Of course we'd stop here. This is Bumpass Hell, named after a human who got too close to a Swartza-controlled mining facility and lost a foot for his trespass. It's one of Seizette's favorite spots. They'll make camp here." Boss turned away from the door and walked along the diamond walls, gazing into their depths. "If we're going to beat Seizette, we have to do it politically. She's reached too many minds with her lies, and a rebellion will look unwarranted to the public—exactly the fuel Seizette would need to be granted emergency power before a vote even takes place. She knows the Head Councilor can ruin the façade of trust she's been weaving with the Truth Seer. I'm sure he's in this diamond somewhere.

Release him, Nathanial, and we have a chance."

Gem put her hand on the wall and closed her eyes. After a minute, she said, "I don't think he's in here."

"Why wouldn't he be?" Nathanial asked. "Does she have another kind of prison?"

"I'm not sure exactly," Gem said. "The Head Councilor is a very powerful sprite. Maybe she needed to deal with him another way."

"You don't think she…" Nathanial gulped. "You don't think she killed him, do you?"

Boss said nothing, but his expression brought no comfort.

Nathanial sulked over to where Aliya lay and joined her on the floor. He put her head onto his lap and brushed her hair.

"I wish you were here," he whispered to her. "You always know what to do."

Hours went by, many filled with Nathanial trying to force the door open with varying forms of his battle blade. Soon the moon bathed its light over the fumarole expulsions, and Nathanial stared, defeated, into the rising steam. He imagined the next day bringing the end to everything he'd fought for. Without the Head Councilor, Seizette would take ultimate authority and send her army into Sanctuary. Nathanial hadn't taken the rings for Aliya, and there was nothing he could do for her now. Seizette would let Aliya die and put him back into the diamond for reconditioning. When he was released a decade later, his mind would no longer be his own, and he would join the Swartza as Seizette's puppet.

Wrapped within his tortured thoughts, it took him a moment to focus on the officer unlocking the door. Boss hurried to hide behind a protruding block of diamond. Nathanial took a few steps back to allow room for the swinging door.

"Our Lady Seizette would like to speak to you," the guard said to Nathanial, and escorted him out into the night.

Entering Seizette's carriage was like coming aboard a first-class train car with presidential decor. Royal shades of red upholstered the couches, and silky curtains hung along the windows. Fruit bouquets exploded with goodies atop all of the end tables, their freshly crafted arrangements stacked tall on silver skewers like edible art pieces.

Nathanial was surprised when the door shut behind him and he was left alone. Then a golden curtain divider opened at the far end of the car and Seizette stepped in with a smile.

"Hello again," she said, as if they were old friends. "Please, have a seat." She gestured toward a couch.

Nathanial's first impulse was to rebel. He was against all that she was and all that she represented. But with a frustrated sigh, he thought of Aliya. Seizette was the only sure way to save her. Nathanial sat down, and the beautiful monster joined him.

"As you know, tomorrow I will be giving my final speech before ultimately being voted in as Head Councilor." She began like it was a normal Sunday afternoon chat they were having. "My first action will be to end the rebellion before it starts another war. I want you to see that I am doing this for the safety and good of my people. Of *our* people." She patted him on the knee. Nathanial clenched his fists. "To express your support, I want you to stand by General Grantz as his new apprentice. I will induct you into my army at the end of tomorrow, and afterward I will save your little friend. Okay?"

Nathanial didn't know what to say. What other options did he have? He couldn't think of any. He allowed his head to bob forward and back, but his mind couldn't comprehend the motion.

"Perfect!" Seizette said, with one more stinging slap on his knee before she stood. "You're going to love joining my legion, Nathanial. Everyone is most fulfilled when serving me directly. How lucky you are." She pulled a cord and the officer came back in. "Put him back with the others for now." Seizette waved to the officer. "Tomorrow we'll arrange something suitable for your new position." She winked at Nathanial before the heavy curtains hid her once again from view.

Nathanial walked slowly back toward the officer and, with his last chance to express rebellion, picked up the fruit bouquet by the door on his way out.

The officer didn't say anything about it, or anything at all, but he kept close on Nathanial's tail as they walked back toward the prisoners' carriage. The chill of the night could not penetrate the numb of his disbelief as he glanced around, in desperate hope of saviors in the woods around them. Nathanial halted when he saw into a carriage window they were passing.

Amaranth was inside, within the warmth of its glow. She was holding a diamond in her hand and something... or someone... stood in front of her. Nathanial took another step to see around the window divider. The Head Councilor appeared glazed within some kind of amber-colored wax. Amaranth put the diamond into the sticky substance by his temple and closed her eyes.

"Hey," prodded the officer behind him, "keep moving."

Nathanial's mind raced for explanations. Once locked firmly back into his carriage, and after he'd seen the officer move away, Nathanial spun on the spot. "Amaranth was the spy! *Is* the spy, is here. She has the Head Councilor."

Boss came out from his hiding spot. "Did you say Amaranth? As in, the Skilla we can thank for freedom of speech?"

"Yes. I know it's hard to believe, but I saw her with the Head Councilor. She has him in… in… some sort of wax!" Nathanial tried not to shout.

"In wax?" Gem asked, the golden sparkles of her nose bunched up.

"Yes. She put a diamond to his head, like the kind that goes in the Truth Seer," Nathanial explained.

Gem pulled a tie string bag from her loose pant pocket, and from it, she took out a diamond. "I'm not sure what the wax has to do with it, but the fact that she has a diamond clarifies things a bit. I was having a hard time reading these spliced memories. They must be manipulated by Skilla imprints."

"What?" Nathanial asked with a tilt of his head.

"As you may know, female Skilla can see images

from your mind when they touch you, or if they can find your vibrations through an object you're touching. The men can send images in the same manner. What most people don't know is that a rare few can do both. I think Amaranth is one of those, and she's using her ability to manipulate the memories in these diamonds."

"She can do that?" Nathanial ogled.

"Yes. That explains these diamonds that you found in Amaranth's room." Gem held up the diamond. "I knew they were spliced memories, the combination of different memories from different sprites. But I didn't know a Skilla had imprinted upon them, as well. Amaranth must be under orders from Seizette to create a public announcement that has such falsehoods that no real memory would suffice. This is only an educated guess, of course. I've not been able to see what's on these diamonds yet. But now that I know it's Amaranth's code and not Seizette's, I can alter my path within these vibrations to better manage cracking their message." Gem turned away to find a quiet corner to sit in with the diamonds.

Boss looked to Nathanial expectantly.

"What?" Nathanial asked.

"What did Seizette say to you?"

Nathanial sucked on his bottom lip. He didn't

want to tell Boss he'd just agreed to change mentors. It might do more than just hurt his feelings.

"Nathanial," Boss pushed, "you need to stop this business where you feel like you need to hide everything from me. You just saw most of my life flash before your eyes. It's a little unfair, don't you think?"

Nathanial almost liked the feeling of Boss's agitation; he so often felt Boss was being unfair and he was getting a taste of his own medicine. But the spite didn't taste good in his mouth, so he complied with a wince. "I agreed to be General Grantz's apprentice in exchange for Aliya's life."

Boss didn't seem at all upset, which kind of bothered Nathanial. Instead, Boss said, "Does that mean you'll be beside her during her address tomorrow?"

Nathanial nodded slowly.

"We could use this to our advantage," Boss said, cupping his chin into his thumb and pointer finger.

"Excuse me?" Nathanial asked.

Boss held the pondering finger up to quiet Nathanial, took a fruit skewer from the bouquet in Nathanial's hand, then found his own corner to retreat into.

Nathanial raised his free arm into the air. "Hypocrite much?" Of course Boss was hiding everything from him. He didn't have the energy to pursue the argument, though, so he returned to Aliya and plopped down beside her. He put a heart-shaped strawberry into his mouth and chewed distractedly.

"Well, at least there's hope I'll see you tomorrow," Nathanial said, and brushed a strand of hair back out of Aliya's eyes. "Even if it means I've sold myself into servitude to do it." He listened to her breathe as he slowly ate through a line of fruit. Then he lay down so that the top of his head touched hers. "Goodnight, Aliya."

THE SWITCH

Being woken up by a tug on his leg in the middle of a dream about losing his foot to a boiling pool of water was not the best way to greet the morning that promised to change the rest of Nathanial's life. He screamed and hit his head on a bump in the diamond wall.

"Ouch!" Nathanial complained to Boss, who stood over him.

"Get up. I want to show you that wing technique I've been dangling over your head," Boss said, and kicked Nathanial's foot again.

Nathanial stood, rubbing his head. "Oh, *now* you decide to show me, now that we're prisoners in a tight, enclosed space. Look at all the good your patience training has done for us."

"Yeah, yeah, just listen. You haven't had to take on many flyers at Sanctuary, and Seizette's army is full of them. You're going to need to know how to spin fight, something I think you'll have a unique advantage with."

Nathanial held his arms out to the confined

quarters and said, "Again, not much room to work with here."

"Your wings," Boss continued, as if Nathanial hadn't spoken, "have alloy edges and tips. Anyone who gets too close to you while you're in full spin could be shredded up like my Uncle Lou." Nathanial lifted a confused brow and Boss explained, "Lawnmower encounter."

"Aw, man." Nathanial winced at the image.

"Now, go ahead and show me your full wing spread," Boss requested.

Nathanial sighed heavily and slowly spread his wings until their tips hit the ceiling and walls around him.

"Yeah. Turn sideways," Boss said, swiveling his finger.

Nathanial turned. His bottom wings were clear of obstacles now, but his top tips still poked the roof.

"Lower the top wings until they're even with the bottom wings, then steady them all straight out from your shoulder blades," Boss instructed.

Nathanial did so. Boss walked up to the nearest wing pair and put the sharp edges into a fork tip alignment.

"That's how you need to hold your wings when you're in full spin," he said, stepping back to view

Nathanial. "I know you can't try it in here, but at least you have a feel for the proper position."

"Are you sure it won't damage my wings if I use them like that?"

"It would be ludicrous for any normal sprite to use their wings in this way. Normally spin fighting is just for clearing an opponent back. But that's where you have the advantage." Boss pushed Nathanial's wings down, put a hand on each of his shoulders, and added with a crooked grin, "You're not normal."

Nathanial knocked Boss's arms away with a laugh. "Shut up."

"But really, Nathanial. You know you're not. It's why Seizette wants you. The very thing she finds disgusting about you—your human traits—are what gives you the edge she wants to use: ultimate control over the battle blade and its abilities. She's quite two-faced, when it suits her."

Nathanial nodded, but something had been nagging at him for a while. "You know, she already has General Grantz. I really don't see why she's so insistent on having me, too."

"Nathanial." Boss pushed his thick hair back from his face. "If she didn't secure you by her side now, you could grow up to lead a rebellion without fear of her watchdog. You could defeat General

Grantz."

Nathanial stared. He couldn't imagine ever fighting someone so powerful.

Gem suddenly appeared beside Boss. "It's done!" She held the tie string bag out to Nathanial. He took it and looked in at all of the diamonds. "Boss says Seizette will have you close to her today. You need to put those in the Truth Seer that she's going to use to broadcast the candidate's closing statements."

"What? Why?" Nathanial asked. How on earth would he manage that?

Unfortunately, the rattling from the carriage door did not allow time for explanations. Boss dived out of sight and Nathanial stuffed the bag into the fold of his armor.

It was the same officer as the night before. "Nathanial, please come with me."

Nathanial allowed himself to be escorted out into the blue morning light. He noticed right away that the front centipede was missing, along with half the Swartza troops.

He was brought over to a two-saddled Odonata with a greenish-blue seahorse head and a neck that attached to a turquoise dragonfly body. The back saddle was already occupied. When the rider's hunter green ponytail turned to reveal a jade green face, he had the instinctive urge to run.

"Good morning, Nathanial," Captain Malik said, with a Cheshire Cat grin.

Nathanial knew this had to be a great moment for Malik. He'd been the first to pursue Nathanial, and with each escape, it only magnified a personal vendetta against him. Nathanial didn't think it fair, considering the prestige Malik had received for his mixed success rate manipulating Nathanial into Swartza service. He was still wearing a fancy captain's uniform, with too many silver fastenings buckling up his turtleneck collar, which meant that he hadn't been fired after his humiliating defeat last time.

Malik extended his hand. "Come on. We're going to the event of the century. It wouldn't be polite to be late."

The officer pushed Nathanial up until he had no other choice but to take Malik's black-gloved hand or fall back onto the rocky ground. He plopped into the front saddle and cringed as Malik slapped the reins that boxed him into place. He wondered what condition Boss and Gem would be in next time he saw them, if he ever saw them again at all.

Soon the smell of rotten eggs faded, and the

fragrance of pine surrounded him on their flight along a dirt path through the evergreens. Suddenly, the tree line ended and Mount Lassen loomed grandly above them. The grays and blacks of a volcanic landscape zoomed desolately beneath the Odonata as they began their long incline.

Up and up they flew toward the ashy peak. As they approached an outcrop of rock, a most unwelcome sight came into view: the headquarters blimp that used to fly high over his home now circled above Mount Lassen. It was quickly blocked from view as they entered a crevasse beneath the rocky outcrop.

The tunnel they flew through was long and dark. Nathanial was growing weary of the constant sound of wind in his ears, but the new commotion echoing toward him from the tunnels' end did not bring relief. It meant they were almost at their dreaded destination.

They exited the tight black rock and entered a cathedral-like space. Nathanial gazed upward in awe: the ceiling stretched with scraped stone toward an oculus, where the foreboding blimp could be spied circling against the blue sky.

When he looked down again, it was to the dismay of seeing two dozen troops guarding a set of arched double doors. One particular guard seemed annoyingly pleased to see them approaching.

"Captain Malik," he said, and took the reins of the Odonata. "We've been expecting you. Lady Seizette has granted you permission to use her exclusive passage. She requests you in her ready chamber."

Malik jumped to the ground, took off his riding gloves, and said, "I will go there immediately. I'll need an escort to keep watch on my company while I'm with her."

Two officers opened the doors for Malik as he headed through without pause, filled with self-importance.

Nathanial rolled his eyes at the scrutinizing gaze of his awaited escort and slid off of the Odonata at a troll's pace. He dragged his feet through the arched doors and down the narrow rock corridor that Malik had long since disappeared into. He didn't stop his heavy strides until he came to another door. This one glittered ridiculously with diamonds. That could only mean one thing.

"Let me guess," he said, and pointed to the decor. "This must be it."

His escort did not seem amused. Nathanial cleared his throat. "Excited about the big election, then?" he asked, rocking on his feet. "Who are you voting for?"

The sprite he addressed exchanged a glance with the one next to him. Nathanial went on with a smirk. "Is there really any other choice besides Seizz—uh, Lady Seizette, though?" He snorted, then added, "No, really, is there another choice?"

The officer licked his lips but kept quiet. The door opened, apparently by itself. Nathanial walked into the room where Malik stood with his hands behind his back. Seizette had a yellow servant girl attending to her.

"Everyone can leave us," Seizette said waving her hand.

The servant girl and Malik passed by Nathanial and the doors closed behind him.

Seizette moved around the room, giving herself final touches as if she'd forgotten Nathanial was there. She put on dangling diamond earrings that accentuated her long sparkling neck and clipped a thick crystalline bracelet to her wrist. Her feminine business suit V-necked to frame a quaint single diamond necklace, and her hair twisted over one shoulder in a spiral ponytail. She finally paused in front of a body-length mirror and admired herself for some time.

"How do I look?" she asked, and smoothed her pale shimmering hands along her hips.

Nathanial was speechless. She looked beautiful,

but that didn't properly reflect what he saw in the mirror. How do you describe a wolf whose attire was way more dazzling than sheep's clothing? Seizette made eye contact with his reflection and smiled. She went over to a covered object on a dresser, picked it up, and brought it to Nathanial. Her high heels clacked as she walked.

"I want you to carry this into the auditorium," she said as he took the object. "Will you do that for me?"

Nathanial nodded, still having trouble finding his voice. "Sure." The word came out as a squeak.

"You can go through that door over there." She pointed to one door of many that framed the hexagonal space. Nathanial wondered where all of them led. "Someone is waiting to show you your place." She smiled and rubbed his cheek.

Going through the motions like the puppet he was being whittled into, Nathanial went through said door and found a magenta sprite in a formal suit waiting for him. "Right this way, sir," the sprite said with a gesture of a white-gloved hand.

At that moment, Nathanial felt an unspoken shift from prisoner to guest. It was more unsettling to be the latter. He now walked through a long hall with beautiful scenic paintings and giant flowers in ornate vases nearly his height.

They stopped at the end, and the usher explained he'd be back for Nathanial momentarily. The usher went through the door and left it open behind him. Nathanial peeked through and saw a stage. Beyond that was a vast number of well-to-do sprites taking seats in a massive curved auditorium. He was backstage at the big event! The usher talked to a sprite who guarded a podium at the center of the stage. Nathanial took the solitary moment to peek under the cover of the object he was tasked with presenting.

His heart attempted to leap from his chest. What luck! Nathanial was holding a Truth Seer! He almost fumbled the device as he backed into a wall and slid out of sight from the door.

Seizette had thought Nathanial no threat and entrusted him with this delivery, surely thinking she was showing off her control. But playing the good little puppet had twisted into his favor. He held the tool for cutting his strings.

Scrambling, he ran over to the nearest vase and ducked down beside it. He searched frantically for the little metallic door on the Truth Seer, found it, slid it open, and pressed the button that sprung the claws loose of their hold. With the diamonds now released, Nathanial turned the Truth Seer upside down into the vase next to him so that all of the diamonds went raining down into its depths. He put the Truth Seer on the floor and rushed to replace the empty sockets with the diamonds from the bag Gem had given him.

"Come on, come on, come on," Nathanial encouraged himself and looked back and forth, confirming the coast was still clear. His hands shook and he fumbled the last diamond.

"Crap!" Nathanial yelled and watched as the diamond tumbled away before stopping at the tip of a boot.

The world elongated around a woman in an elegant black gown. She bent down to retrieve the diamond. It was Amaranth. She stood again, examined the crystal in her hand, then said, "I have a better one." She pulled a diamond from a small chest pocket and handed it to Nathanial.

Nathanial looked at it, and then to her. He remembered Gem saying that Amaranth could put images into the diamond even if they weren't true, and that she was most likely working to do such a thing on Seizette's behalf. He gulped, uncertain of what to do.

Amaranth looked as though she was about to say more, but her eyes darted to the auditorium door.

Nathanial followed her gaze and saw the usher

returning. With the choice of using her diamond or leaving a suspicious empty slot in the Truth Seer, he quickly put hers into place, pushed the button to secure the lot, and covered the device. His heart plunged like a boulder into his stomach. What had he just done?

The usher stopped before Amaranth and greeted her with a slight bow.

"Ah, Lady Amaranth. You may follow me, along with the young gentleman," he said, and turned to lead them onto the stage.

The usher took Amaranth to her seat in the front row. Nathanial's heart cringed to see her company: Codfear Brack, the head of Big Lyso; Cyron, who had kept Aliya as a prisoner; and Malik, who hated Nathanial on principle. It gutted Nathanial to see Cyron had also, like Malik, benefitted from a promotion at his and Aliya's expense. If they were the sort whom Amaranth was politically on par with, then it confirmed his mistake: putting her diamond into the Truth Seer was surely sabotage against the ones Gem had altered.

The usher showed Nathanial to the podium on stage and pointed to a diamond circle the size of the Truth Seer's base. Nathanial kept his head low and tried not to feel the heat of the auditorium's eyes beaming into him.

"How exciting for you." The usher smiled at Nathanial. "Have you thought about what you are going to say?"

"Huh?" Nathanial didn't understand.

"When you put the Truth Seer in the circlet, it will go live. You will be the first thing millions of sprites from all over the world will see at this event."

Nathanial froze. He was pretty sure his heart had just stopped beating.

The usher seemed to take the response as excitement and added, "I know! It's wonderful, isn't it? You must feel so honored to be part of this historic moment. Having you here sends a good message."

The message presumably being that Nathanial, a human turned sprite, had not been persecuted by the Swartza like the Head Councilor had claimed, no, not at all. In fact, Nathanial was openly supporting the Swartza. Look at him as he starts the Truth Seer's live broadcast at this historical event! And then he will go stand beside General Grantz as his new apprentice.

Nathanial felt sick. Could Gem's diamonds possibly counter the inevitable meaning of this moment? What had Amaranth added to the equation? Could he recognize that last diamond and pull it without anyone noticing?

The panic was suffocating, and the usher was looking at him expectantly. Nathanial twisted the device into place and watched the silver arms spread wide.

For a moment he stared at the glowing disseminator of doom, imagining all of the sprites who might be looking at him from all over the planet. He wondered if there was something he might say to them, something to make them understand the weight of the decision their vote would have on so many oppressed lives.

"It's okay," the usher said, and pulled Nathanial away, as if in understanding of the gaping silence. "The announcer will be out momentarily. Let me show you your place."

THE TRUTH WILL SET YOU FREE

Nathanial was in place at the edge of the stage. The delegates were settling in. Students in their Swartza High uniforms filled the top rows of the balcony, and Nathanial kept skimming the rows for Jozy. He'd never heard if she made it through the trials or not. But the students were too far away, and he couldn't make out individual faces.

Finally, the introductions began. Nathanial couldn't wait to see who was running against Seizette. She often spoke as if she were the only candidate, but he knew that couldn't be true. After all, you couldn't have a vote with just one candidate. So when the feeble Doctor Gustoes was announced to the podium, Nathanial couldn't help but feel disappointment. The doctor needed a box to stand on in order to be seen above the podium and the white hair that poured out from his wrinkly ears was combed into his twisted beard.

"Good day," the doctor said in a high strained voice. "I'm pleased to be here as a candidate for

Head Councilor."

Nathanial could see the Truth Seer shining bright on the podium in front of Doctor Gustoes. He looked around to see if there were any TVs that reflected what the world was seeing, but there was no such luck.

"You all know my qualifications. I've been a healer at Rugsboth medical factory since I popped my colors half a century ago. I'd be happy to turn my healing abilities to mend the rift in our broken economy. Thank you." And with that short riff, he took a seat in the front row with Amaranth.

Sporadic clapping echoed momentarily in the room before the announcer returned to the podium. "Thank you, Doctor Gustoes," he said politely.

Nathanial rolled his eyes. Was that really it? That was Seizette's competition? How obviously rigged.

"Now I have the honor to present the High Educator of Swartza High, Governess of Swartzaville, and former Queen of… *us!*" Everyone laughed. "Lady Seizette!"

The room roared into a cheer. There was an obvious bias for her. It was like everyone's favorite superstar, sports player, and musician had just entered the room, all at once.

Seizette entered through the same door

Nathanial had. She waved to the crowd as she passed him by. General Grantz entered seconds after and stopped beside Nathanial. The close proximity only amplified the extreme height difference, and made Nathanial feel quite lame.

"Thank you," Seizette said to the steady round of applause. "Thank you." She let the enthusiasm roll over her like an embrace. When it naturally died down, she finally began her speech. "Thank you all for selecting me as a candidate for Head Councilor. To have this chance to protect spritekind once again, not as a queen but as an elected official, will make this journey all the more meaningful."

"Why even vote? She's already accepting the position," Nathanial mumbled.

"As Head Councilor, if you should choose me." She laughed as if any other idea were absurd, and the crowd giggled, too. "I will restore balance to our society and propel us into the next great advancement. You've all seen the wondrous success of Swartzaville. We do not hide in the shadows. We do not fear that any human will tread on us. We are strong, and I am ready to take this stand and remind you just how capable you all are."

More applause. Nathanial found Larix in the crowd. He, too, was clapping—so much for his change of mind at Sanctuary.

Nathanial felt hopeless. The diamonds Gem had provided him didn't seem to be doing anything, and who even knew what Amaranth was trying to pull with hers? The Truth Seer was just glowing in place. It wasn't zapping Seizette into oblivion or anything. It must have been that last diamond he put in. It had ruined everything. Whatever Gem had tried to do was being countered by Amaranth.

But then, just as he was resigning himself to a Swartza life, the announcer walked over and whispered something in Seizette's ear. Whatever it was, she looked straight at Nathanial, and she looked angry. He put on his best innocent face but her gaze burned right through it. Seizette tried to remove the Truth Seer from its place, nonchalantly, but it wouldn't budge.

"Thank you, Lady Seizette," the announcer said.

Seizette tried to smile and wave while moving away from the podium, but then she doubled her pace over to General Grantz. "Destroy it, then come find me," she said to him and disappeared through the backstage door.

The general pulled out his axe and the room gasped. Nathanial thought it a good idea to stop something that Seizette wanted, so he grabbed hold of the general's belt loop… to no effect. Amaranth suddenly moved in front of the general and put her hand on his temple. He froze, arm still high in the air.

Nathanial was touching the general and he could see the images Amaranth plunged into the general's brain. He was back on the mushroom with his love. The soldiers surrounded them. The general pulled out his battle blade. Nathanial remembered the sudden images of death all around him, including the general's beloved, from inside the diamond the day before.

This time, however, he saw Seizette enter the fray, with Amaranth at her side. She shot a barrage of diamonds at the general. They sunk into his chest and froze him, petrified into place. Then she walked over to Jessabelle.

"Please. Why are you doing this?" Jessabelle asked, rubbing her protruding pregnant belly. "I thought you were kind. You told me I could leave with him."

Seizette breathed out a laugh. "You are so naïve. Do you think anyone is allowed to leave my service? Swartza allegiance is for life. I shouldn't have to tell you that. You should know it in your heart."

Seizette wiped a tear from Jessabelle's cheek and left her hand cradled there until diamonds grew out from every pore in her body. Seizette pushed the newly formed crystal block into the earth, burying it deep out of site, and brushed her hands off. Then she walked to the still-frozen general and put her hand on the battle blade until it glowed red. She backed away and calmly watched. She didn't bother to warn her troops, who were waiting dutifully near the general when the explosion happened.

"Make him forget I was ever here, and have him see Jessabelle dead among the others," Seizette said to Amaranth. Amaranth approached the general and placed her hand on his temple.

Nathanial stumbled backward out of the images and saw they were still on the stage of the auditorium. General Grantz's axe shrank down into knife form.

"I'm sorry," Amaranth said to him. "I had to do horrible things to protect my cover. Seizette tapped your battle blade. It was her power that overloaded it that day. She created the self-loathing in you to channel your anger into a weapon. I hope this truth will give you what you need to let go of your anger and remember who you are. You did not kill your love, but Seizette ultimately did. Now your daughter is in danger from that same curse that took Jessabelle. Do not waste any more of your life fighting needlessly. If you must fight, fight for your daughter."

Nathanial was transfixed. Did this mean what he thought it meant? He racked his brain to remember. Hadn't Mataunte called her sister "Jessabelle" in the memories he'd seen while in the diamond at Swartza High? How did he not catch this sooner? Jessabelle was Aliya's mother, and that meant—General Grantz was her father! His stomach lurched at the realization. The lengths Seizette went to in order to manipulate people were sickeningly vast. Seizette was trying to do the same to him! Manipulating him by holding Aliya's life ransom.

With Aliya in his thoughts, he turned to march out the door. He was going to find Seizette and stop her madness once and for all. He would demand she release Aliya from the curse, or instead he would become the weapon she so badly wanted him to be—only his blade point would be focused on her.

He ran all the way back to the ready room and only stopped when he saw the door was cracked open. He peeked into the room and saw Seizette activating another Truth Seer.

"Truth Seer, show me the live broadcast," she said, hands on hips.

A bright light scattered up along the walls

and ceiling until the prismatic colors shaped into memories from Nathanial's life. His mouth dropped, knowing that countless sprites were watching from all over the world. They were witness to his sickness, his wishes upon every birthday cake for his health, his mother always there to console him. They saw Gem granting his wish to be healthy by turning him into a sprite, and then the memory shifted into a perspective that was not his own, and he understood. These were spliced memories that Gem had sorted out, and there was more she wanted the public to see.

Nathanial watched the truth of Gem's abduction. She was surrounded by Swartza troops as Seizette encased her within a diamond block, reminding Gem that no one gets to change their birth blood, especially not a pathetic factory whose place is to serve spritekind.

"Shut up," Seizette said through gritted teeth. "This shouldn't be happening."

But the memories persisted, and now they were from the Head Councilor. He was being told about Gem's disappearance and the likelihood of it being the Swartza who took her.

"Seizette's supporters have been slowly eking their way back into power," the Head Councilor said dolefully. "The Crossing Treaty left her with more opportunity than we realized. She's been able to politically outmaneuver us for awhile now. We can't let her get away with this."

Then another day through the Head Councilor's memory was on display. A sprite, who looked to be his bodyguard, was frantic, saying, "Please, sir, you don't understand. She's told everyone that you are refusing to step down. She is sending Swartza enforcers." A knock sounded at the door. "That's them now! You must go out the secret way!"

"This is ridiculous," the Head Councilor said. "I sent out a formal statement accepting the public's will. She can't do this."

"She *is* doing this," his bodyguard insisted. "You must escape and find the evidence you need to regain the public's support. We all lose if she takes you here. Those loyal to you wait to take you to safety. Go *now*! I will make sure you are not followed."

Then, there it was, for every sprite in every town to see: the evidence. Proof that the factory-friendly plants did not collapse but were instead forced under by Seizette. The documents with clear green arrows rising beside Grit-the-Gook Pro screamed brightly, next to the red arrow of Thatcherville's Grit-the-Gook profits.

When the images shifted again, to Seizette

capturing the Head Councilor, Nathanial had to cover his mouth to prevent an audible gasp. Delegate Larix stood with Seizette in the centipede car.

"My diamond may be compromised in his case," she said to him. "Will you put him in that beautiful amber of yours for me? I still want to display him at Swartza High."

"No!" The real Seizette screamed and threw the Truth Seer across the room. It shattered against the wall into dozens of crystalline fragments. She grabbed an overcoat off a hook and exited the far door. Nathanial followed her. She was moving fast. He saw only her coattails at the end of each new hall he entered. She was trying to escape.

Nathanial cautiously approached the large doors that led to the vast room where troops had been stationed that morning. They were all flying Odonatas out into the canyon exit, as an escort to Seizette. Nathanial spread his wings and flew after them. He didn't stop until he'd exited the mountain and landed high on a rock. The entourage floated down the ashy slope. Nathanial didn't know how long he could give chase, or if it was safe for him to stay so close on their tail, but this was as vulnerable as he'd ever seen Seizette. If he could get help, this could be the opportunity to stop her before she regrouped. He closed his eyes and felt to see if Sidian was around.

Sidian quickly swooped down from a nearby treetop to meet Nathanial.

"Hey, Sid! Boy, am I glad to see you!" Nathanial jumped onto his neck. "Think we can get in front of them? It looks like they're heading back to Bumpass Hell. We should get there first and free the others."

Sidian clicked his beak and flapped his wings.

They passed high over Seizette and her escort. It wasn't long before he smelled the rotten egg odor of Bumpass Hell. Once past the trees, Nathanial gaped at the chaotic sight among the mudpots. Sanctuary hadn't waited to be invaded—they came to do the invading, and they appeared to be doing it with style.

Many of Seizette's troops had already been wrapped up in grass cocoons, spid-o-matic webs, and root cages. Sanctuary's sprites were having the hardest time with the transmogrified beasts, but with amazing team work and coordination, the sprites seemed to be herding most of them into a hollowed out tree stump.

Nathanial hooted in laughter. When he was at Swartza High, he'd always thought it a terrible idea that they refused to practice their nature abilities.

They always thought themselves above it, and now they were getting whipped by it—literally. Bunny was whipping one of them with a blade of grass and then hogtied him with it.

Mila flew up beside Nathanial on Ori's back. She was finally wearing some armor, something tough and black and resembling scale mail. Ori even had a little helmet that was flame orange to match her bright head feathers.

"Where've you been?" Mila asked. "Can't you see we're catching some Swartza scum over here?" She waved toward the numerous Skilla on bird back that dove down and scooped up the transmogrified creatures, dumped them off into the deep woods, and swooped back in again.

"I see that," Nathanial said, amazed at the cavalry. "Who're your friends?"

"Not just friends. My parents are over there, sharing my dad's ride so I could take Ori." She pointed at a male and a female sprite, both purple and clad in scale mail, who were capturing foul beasts. "After what happened to you and Aliya at the debate, I made a few calls. We were on our way not long after you. Kia called in a heap ton of chipmunks for most of Sanctuary to ride, and even Dusty got some of his kin to join us with their blue jays."

"Good, we need all the help we can get. I'm hoping to catch the queen of these scum. She's headed this way. Where's Boss?"

Mila looked down and pointed to the blue streak that knocked down any troop that was near it. "There," she said, "being an army of one."

Nathanial flew off Sidian's back and landed near the spot. He ran into the cascade of bodies and yelled, "Boss!"

Boss froze, fist reared back to punch, and the officer he was about to hit slowly backed away before turning and sprinting into the woods.

"What?" Boss said, pushing his hair back out of his face.

"I did it! The Truth Seer showed the public the truth, for real this time. Seizette's almost here. She's on the run, trying to regroup with her force." Nathanial said.

"We need to head her off. Take me to her."

Nathanial flew beside Boss, back toward the dirt trail that led up to the volcanic peak. As he passed a group of Sanctuary defenders, he heard a little voice call, "Hey! There goes Nat!" Nathanial almost stopped to see Spassel, but he didn't want the little guy getting involved with what he was about to face. Bunny and Gem, however, jumped aboard a couple of mice and soon trailed behind them. Mila and Ori were following from the sky, with Sidian flying alongside.

"How many troops does she have with her?" Boss asked as they continued into the deepening wood.

"A couple dozen," Nathanial said. "But the general could be here with the rest soon."

"We need to flank them," Boss said, and he pointed for Bunny to hide on the left of the trail, then to Gem to hide on the right. "I want you in the trees up there. I'll be opposite you. Mila, you and Sidian stay hidden just ahead. Sidian, let Nathanial know when they're approaching."

Sidian cawed and everyone got into position. Nathanial's heart raced in anticipation of the moment—or maybe it was the intense connection he was sharing with Sidian. His vision distorted, and he saw through Sidian's wide-angle eyes.

Seizette appeared at the trail's head, joined by a couple of daunting figures. Both Cyron and Malik flanked her, and they were aboard scorpions. Apparently, there had been no need to transmogrify them.

Nathanial shook Sidian's point of view out of his mind and signaled to Boss that they were on approach. He didn't know how to signal that scorpions accompanied them, but he hoped his terrified expression gave away some sense of it.

As the troops fell into the center of their ambush, Boss flew down in front of them with his hand up. "Stop," he said commandingly. "You are surrounded. Give yourselves up and the law may be forgiving… to the troops, anyway."

"We are the law," Captain Malik said imperiously from atop his beast.

"Sorry, has no one told you the news?" Boss asked, feigning sorrow. "Your secret's out. No one wants you anymore. Without the people's support, you have no power." Boss had been speaking to Malik, but his eyes found Seizette's by the end. She was fuming. "Looks like you're getting that Fourth Rebellion you were hoping for. Only I don't think it's going to turn out how you expected."

"Kill him," Seizette said.

Insanity broke loose.

THE CRACKING

A funnel of troops zeroed in on Boss's position as Bunny and Gem sent mouse teeth into scorpion tails before they had a chance to strike. Nathanial pulled out his battle blade and dove towards Boss's position, all the while checking Sidian's vision to keep an eye on Seizette. Amazingly, Seizette did not run. She appeared to be enjoying the scene too much.

This was the strangest fight Nathanial had ever been a part of. Boss was right: these troops could fly, and it made for a staggering defense strategy. They took flight whenever their attack position was compromised, and they swooped back in from odd angles. Then they would spin wildly, forcing an opponent backwards, before they would thrust in with long sharpened blades.

Nathanial had his battle blade in blunt staff form; he didn't want to kill anybody. They'd all been brainwashed by Seizette. Maybe they would come around if she was brought down. He just needed to immobilize them, but they weren't making it easy.

Just when Nathanial thought he had a handle on blocking the crazy attacks, Malik jumped free of his downed scorpion and ordered the troops to focus on Boss. He then flanked Nathanial, with Cyron rounding the opposite side. Nathanial glared at the dirty tactic that he'd seen used all too often at Swartza High. He'd managed to best Malik one-on-one, but he'd never beaten Cyron. In fact, Cyron had been haunting his nightmares ever since he first ripped Aliya away from him, then crumpled him to the ground with barely a push.

Nathanial shook his battle blade staff. It transformed into a spear with a blade on each end.

Malik laughed. "I'm glad to see I still have that effect on you."

"Don't flatter yourself," Nathanial said, having hoped the spear would intimidate his attackers to back off. "You know I can take you. Isn't that why you brought this troll for backup?"

Cyron growled with a sneer.

"Look." Nathanial attempted to compromise. "Seizette's through. There's no use in this."

"I didn't serve Seizette when I met you. I only joined her for the opportunity to continue my pursuit of you. I would see you fall even if she does," Malik said, and pulled his sword from its sheath.

Nathanial felt Sidian's urge to come to rescue him, but as soon as he took flight, he was bulldozed by a Swartza raven. Bunny and Gem were wrestling down the last scorpion, and Boss was highly occupied. Nathanial was going to have to handle these jerks on his own.

Malik lunged at Nathanial. He quickly parried and glanced behind him to see Cyron opening up a net.

"Hey," Nathanial said, pointing at him with his weapon, "don't even think about it! Not fair."

"Was it fair when you took my livelihood away from me?" Cyron jeered, his seaweed complexion flushing. "Your actions forced me into negotiations with the High Queen of Swartza. Thanks to you, I now serve her, away from my beloved sea. I hate the dry air of this place as much as I hate you. Before the end, I will make you wish you'd never laid eyes on Aliya."

Malik swung at Nathanial, and he blocked. Cyron threw his net, and Nathanial dived out from under it. Malik lunged to cut Nathanial's head from his shoulders, but he scrambled up from the ground just in time. Cyron reeled his net back in, then readied to cast it again. These guys were too fast, too experienced, and Nathanial felt sluggish in comparison.

He transformed his spear into a sword, feeling confident from Boss's training, then had an idea from the general's demonstration in the woods. He pulled a shield out from the hilt of his sword, and it was just in time for Malik's blade to come crashing down upon it.

Nathanial heaved a deep breath: too close. He swished his sword at Cyron, who closed in on his other side. Their attacks were getting even quicker. Nathanial was losing. He felt desperate. It was time to try something he'd never tried before. He was a cornered rat.

Nathanial combined the sword and shield back into a single knife and sheathed it into his chest holster. Then he took a breath, pulled in his arms, and twisted like a tornado on the spot. He pushed his wings straight out into their tight spin fighting position. His acceleration seemed unnatural, as if the power in the battle blade was aiding his speed. He felt resistance against his wings, he knew he had hit something or someone, but he did not stop. A loud whistle screamed from the cutting air and the blood in his head swam. Nathanial fell to his knees from the overwhelming dizziness.

He slowly opened his eyes and, once the world stopped spinning, saw the shredded net around him. He was almost afraid to look up, in case the lawnmower analogy had taken effect—but he needed to see into the silence.

Malik and Cyron stood stock-still. The chests of their fancy suits were shredded, their hands raised and scratchy. Malik's sword was on the ground, its tip severed clean off.

Nathanial made eye contact with Boss in the halted crowd. His grin shone bright like a newborn sun.

Seizette glared at Nathanial from her lofty position of safety behind the fray. He could see her longing to control him.

Then, all eyes turned to an approaching shadow: General Grantz and his flying tank of a bear landed behind Seizette, dwarfing her and her mount.

"Finally," Seizette said, in almost bored relief. "Could you end this for me already, my dear? I grow tired of it all."

She jumped down from the bedazzled Odonata and walked confidently, knowing that the general was at her back. She stopped at Boss, put a finger on his cheek, and said, "You were a fool to deny me. You could have been everything to me, and that would have been everything to you."

She pushed her finger so it was more of a slap across his face. Then she continued over to

Nathanial. "I'm still not sure I'm ready to give up on you," she said gently. "Look at your potential. You haven't even blossomed your colors. I think I'll save you for later."

Seizette put her hands on Nathanial's shoulders and he felt his body solidifying from the inside out. He screamed as the sensation of a trillion microscopic knives hurdled through his bloodstream. Diamonds erupted from his skin, his vision blurring into blackness, and just when the crystals threatened to choke out his breath, the pain stopped.

Oddly, when his screaming stopped, it was replaced by another's. The knives left him and his vision returned. He saw that the general's battle blade was now a silver and gold glove upon Seizette's shoulder. All of the diamonds had traveled off Nathanial's skin and onto hers.

"This… isn't… possible!" Seizette struggled with the words.

Nathanial stumbled backward. He watched in astonishment as Seizette became a block of diamond. But the crystals weren't finished… they kept spreading.

"Stop," Nathanial said to the general. "You can stop now." He tried to remove the general's hand from Seizette's shoulder, but it was one with the diamond. It spread up through the general's arm. "No!" Nathanial cried.

"Don't mourn for me," the general said. "Where I took life, let me now give it. Let me save my daughter. Let me have redemption."

"Do you even know who your daughter is?" Nathanial asked, still pulling at the solidified arm. "It's Aliya! The girl I've been trying to save this whole time. You tried to give me a ring to save her. Did Seizette show you how amazing she is when she told you about us? Did you see how beautiful, and smart, and brave she is? You should meet her! Let go!"

A small smile formed on the general's lips. "I must do this. I am the only one powerful enough to stop her. It is good to know Aliya has you in my stead. Thank you, Nathanial Thatcher."

Like a flash freeze, the diamond finished its consumption, and everything fell into a cold silence.

Boss came up to Nathanial and pulled him back from the large diamond block. "Step away," he said softly.

The ground began to shake. The earthquake shook the sprites off their feet and the Swartza ravens fled, cawing high into the skies. The diamond began to crack.

"Get down!" Boss screamed, and forced Nathanial to the ground.

The air exploded outward with a bang and glittering shards of crystalline dust snowed down upon the scene.

Everyone stood up slowly. They were all dusted with the clear, glittering powder. The troops looked confused. One of them asked Malik, "What are our orders, Captain?"

Malik wiped the dust from his brow. "I'm not your captain." He gave Nathanial one long, defeated look and then moved on, into the woods.

For one moment, Cyron tensed and glared at Nathanial as if considering another attack. Nathanial placed his hand to his chest, where the battle blade was stowed. Cyron sneered hatefully at Nathanial and turned away.

"Should we stop them?" Nathanial asked Boss.

"Not now," Boss said knowingly. "We need the power of the Council to detain them. That will be back in our hands soon enough, and their prosecution will be swift."

Without leadership, the troops decided amongst themselves to head back to the volcano, where officials might still wait with instructions.

Bunny and Gem gathered around Nathanial and hugged him. Bunny wiped a tear from Nathanial's cheek. Mila swooped down with Ori, a dozen Skilla on bird-back hanging over them in the sky. Mila said, "You're not going to believe what just happened!"

"Where've you been?" Nathanial asked. He hadn't seen her in the fight.

"I thought you needed reinforcements!" Mila exclaimed, pointing to the birds in the sky. "But here I find you, just hugging it out in the middle of nowhere, all by yourselves. Anyway, you need to come back to Bumpass Hell."

Gem and Bunny boarded their mice and Sidian glided down to pick up Boss and Nathanial. They all followed Mila and Ori back to Bumpass Hell.

The unbelievable thing that Mila was so excited about was immediately evident as they landed amongst the rubble of the centipede cars; the diamond prison was no more and the centipede had fled into the woods from the look of its tracks. Sprites covered in diamond dust were walking around, finding loved ones from Sanctuary and asking what had happened.

Boss locked eyes with one of the sparkling lost sprites. She had the complexion of flower pollen and her eyes were hazel starbursts. She smiled brilliantly when she saw Boss approaching her. He took her hands and pulled her into an embrace.

"Conrad," she said softly. "Is it really you?"

"Sarah," Boss said, and touched her cheek.

She almost cried. "You remember me?"

"I didn't remember for a long time, but eventually the pieces started coming back to me. When I realized it was you who had saved me from Seizette, I went looking for you. I searched all around that port town where we'd met, hoping you'd find your way back. What happened to you?"

"When I left home to see if what you had told me was true—that I was living in a bubble outside of normal time—I didn't realize I couldn't return. When that hit me, I was only further beside myself imagining that I'd never see you again. Then I had an epiphany: if it could be true that my town was moving slowly outside of normal time, then the fairy tales could be true, too. And I started wishing. Every conceivable way to wish, I wished.

"It wasn't until I found an old water well that I found a wish sprite who would speak to me. I told her about you, and I was astonished that she knew who you were. You were famous in the sprite world! You were leading a rebellion, but you had been captured. She said that new laws were strangling her kind, making it more difficult to grant the sort of wish I needed to find you, but she was a rebel and so she turned me into a sprite despite the restrictions. Not just any kind of sprite, either, but the sort that would be easily overlooked in the halls of Swartza: a yellow servant with abilities to go unnoticed. She sent me into the hive where you were being held and gave me the plan to aid your escape.

"I was able to get you to the extraction point, but to keep you from being hunted I needed to do one last thing. I backtracked and made it look like you had jumped from a window by smashing out the pane of glass in your room. They would presume that your body was washed down the river that raged below.

"Seizette discovered me at the scene. The wish sprite knew Seizette would probe my mind, and so she had had a Skilla imprint a vision of your death in my mind. It worked. It convinced Seizette that you were dead. But we did not anticipate that she would then lock me into the diamond out of her frustration and hate."

Boss shook his head and held her again. "I'm so sorry you had to go through that." He pulled back and then kissed her gently.

Nathanial saw this and couldn't help his thoughts landing on Aliya. He ran to where her carriage should have been but found a mound of dust instead. Ms. Collette sat crouched within it,

Aliya in her arms.

"How is she?" Nathanial asked, and took a knee beside her.

"I think she's going to be alright," Ms. Collette said. "Thanks to you, Nathanial."

"Well, it wasn't just me," Nathanial said, and then tilted his head at her. "You just called me Nathanial. Sprites at Sanctuary call me Nathan."

Ms. Collette nodded. "I've been watching you since the day you pulled Aliya off the *Argosy*. I thought she was trapped forever, until the day you came along. You have been her liberator, defender, and friend. Thank you."

"Who are you?" Nathanial asked as he tried to figure it out. Then he slapped his hand to his forehead. He should have recognized her from the blood memory, but the hair and glasses and her young age had definitely thrown him off. "You're Mataunte!"

Ms. Collette laughed and said, "Aliya is the only one who's ever called me that."

"You taught Aliya everything she knows about the sprites. You even taught her to hate them."

"I needed her to have her guard up when she entered this world. You both saw what little regard sprites have for human rights, and that's a prejudice many have, no matter their political affiliation."

"I understand," Nathanial said. "But I'm not sure she will when she finds out you're a sprite. She might call you a hypocrite."

Ms. Collette smiled and nodded. "That will be fine with me."

With a gasp, as if she'd reemerged from water, Aliya sat up and began to cough.

"You're okay," Nathanial said excitedly. "You're going to be okay now."

Aliya turned to Nathanial and gave him a quick embrace. "I saw everything," she said. "In your memories. You saw my mother, my real mother, and how she was cursed by Seizette."

"I know," Nathanial said. "I'm so sorry I didn't tell you. I didn't know how to tell you that the man who raised you wasn't your father... and I've learned something new, too... about your real father."

"What? My *real* father?"

"General Grantz," he said hesitantly. "You know, the guy you saw in the block of diamond at Swartza High?" Aliya's eyes widened and he hurried to ease her fear. "But everything he did was out of grief of losing your mother. He just saved me from being encased in the diamond myself, and he turned Seizette's own evil trick against her! I think he did what he had to do to release everyone from her, and more specifically, to stop the curse. Aliya, he said he did it to save you."

"Did what?" Aliya asked, unsure.

Nathanial sighed. "He sacrificed himself to take down Seizette. He said he was the only one powerful enough to do it. I tried to stop him, but he seemed to think it was the only way. I don't know why, Aliya. I'm so sorry."

"What?" Aliya shook her head. "But how did he even know about me?"

"It was Amaranth," Nathanial explained. "She showed him the truth. Showed him that Seizette cursed your mother and you. It was enough to change him."

"So Amaranth's not a spy?"

"Oh, she is. But, like, in a double agent sort of way that benefits our side."

Aliya took a moment to digest the news, then she looked to Ms. Colette. "Mataunte," she said softly. "It's you, isn't it? I saw you in the memories, and you called me 'minette' at school. I wasn't sure if it was just a coincidence then... but now I know."

"Yes, minette, it is me," Ms. Colette said. "I've had to glamor myself to hide from Swartza. It's an easy thing for a love sprite."

Aliya hugged Ms. Collette and laughed. "You being a sprite explains a lot."

Ms. Collette nodded shyly.

"Now you know the truth," Ms. Collette said. "And I want you to know the whole truth: the man who raised you as his own is a cousin from your father's side. Your father's brother had a family, and it was his descendants whom I brought you to when you were orphaned. That way you could know a piece of yourself, through them."

"And you're my aunt on my mom's side," Aliya said, a small tear running down her cheek. "So I know that piece of myself, too. And that I was always surrounded by family."

"And you always will be. They may be your cousins by blood, but they will always be your sister and papa by heart. I told them for years that I was watching over you, and that I would one day be able to bring you home again. Thanks to Nathanial's efforts, I will be able to keep that promise. Whenever you're ready."

The three of them embraced in relief.

Mila walked over and said, "Another hug-fest!" She crossed her arms and shook her head.

Nathanial got to his feet and said to Mila, "Thanks for all your help, even if it felt like tough love most the time. You really pushed me to defend myself at that debate. Looks like I convinced you to act, though, eh?"

"Yeah, well, if the Head Councilor didn't get captured, we might have had a chance at avoiding a rebellion…"

Nathanial lifted a brow, waiting to see if she was really going to be this stubborn.

"…but, you did show some pretty terrifying evidence to the contrary. Kind of lit a fire underneath all of Sanctuary. And I'm glad you interfered in the end, so… yeah, good job."

Nathanial had never seen Mila admit defeat before. He was spared having to gather an appropriate response by Spassel running up to them.

"Hey, can I have a hug too?" Spassel asked, jumping in.

Nathanial laughed and clobbered Spassel into a hug.

"Oh, brother." Mila rolled her eyes and Nathanial forced her into a group embrace. She fell into it without resistance.

The whole gang—Boss, Sarah, Bunny, Gem, and Phlegm—watched from beside a burbling blue mudpot with amusement.

"Don't laugh or I'll tackle all of you next," Nathanial warned.

"Oh, that's enough to buy my silence," Phlegm said, zipping his lips.

Nathanial felt like no wrong could befall them at that moment—until he saw an uncertain sight approaching from down the road.

Amaranth and the Head Councilor came, alongside Delegate Larix. Nathanial and his group walked over to Boss. Amaranth and hers stopped to meet them all.

"Larix apologizes for his momentary lapse in judgment and needed no persuading to release the Head Councilor from his amber," Amaranth said with a single lifted brow.

"I was under the influence of Lady Seizette," Larix admitted. "She threatened my family."

"She threatened us all," the Head Councilor said. "We have quite a mess to clean up from her wake." He looked around heavily, to all of the cages filled with Swartza that scattered the alien landscape of sulfur-stained stone and rainbow pools of acidic water.

"Do you think the public will come around easily?" Boss asked.

"I think the memory projections from the Truth Seer will have been a great help to that effect."

"How did the Truth Seer get your memories, Head Councilor? You were never in the diamond, were you?" Nathanial asked. It was something that had been bugging him. If the Head Councilor hadn't been in the diamond, there was no way for those memories to be downloaded.

"That was me," Amaranth admitted. "I've been working on cracking diamond code for over a century. I had a blank diamond on me from Lady Seizette's Truth Seer pack. She had given me the device personally, knowing that I was headed for Sanctuary, but she didn't believe I would spy for her willingly after I'd sided with the rebels the last time. She hoped I wouldn't notice the transmitter that would do the spying for her. I wasn't worried, however, as I knew the device would come in more useful to us than to her. We needed to know what she was telling the public, and how the device worked. And it did work in our favor: I snuck into the coach where the Head Councilor was ambered up and extracted his memories into the blank diamond. That's the gem I gave you in the hall, Nathanial. It's a good thing you trusted me."

Nathanial half-smiled at the guilt of not actually trusting her. He had seen her with the Head Councilor in amber and thought she was doing something nefarious.

"What surprises me is the magnitude of this rubble," Amaranth added. "We were told by the retreating troops that the general had turned on Seizette, but I can't see how that would affect the diamond that was here."

"I think I can explain that," Gem said. "But first I have a question for you, Amaranth."

"Go on," Amaranth said.

"Why were your imprints on the spliced diamonds of the Truth Seer that Seizette sent with you into Sanctuary? What were you trying to manipulate in them?"

Amaranth took a deep breath, realizing that the question sounded like an accusation that she was still a spy for Seizette. But she calmly answered, without spite. "Seizette gave me the Truth Seer and the accompanying diamonds for more reasons than the one I just stated. She also wanted me to see that she didn't need me anymore. To see that she had replaced me with another Skilla. She had been using another of my kind to imprint voice propaganda onto memories. At this point, that is all that was overlaid onto the real images.

"The imprints you are asking me about, the ones of my own, were experiments. I wanted to see if I could remove the voice overlays, but I also wanted to be sure that the images were not false. I think, given time, we would have seen completely fabricated propaganda of both voice and image through the Truth Seer. But, thankfully, that's something we do not need to worry about now."

Gem nodded, seemingly satisfied with the answer. "To explain the devastation of the diamond around us, let me first explain what I discovered while trapped inside the diamond. It felt alive—which is odd, because when I grew quartz crystal before I became a wish sprite, the crystals I grew were never alive, and they were not a part of me once I set them into nature. But the diamond… it *was* a part of Seizette, and the people she imprisoned gave her vitality. It made her immortal."

There was a quiet gasp within the group.

"That's why she kept the diamond prison close to her," Gem added. "And why it has crumbled along with her."

"We didn't even properly understand what a threat she was," the Head Councilor marveled.

"That's what General Grantz meant," Nathanial realized in open sorrow. "He said that he was the only one powerful enough to stop her. Not only did he need to take out Seizette, but he also needed to destroy the source of her power. I can't even imagine the amount of strength it took for him to do that."

"An unimaginable amount of power indeed," the Head Councilor said. "She had all the time in the universe to plot her way back into control.

We're lucky we had some new players in the game to help us out this time. You, Nathanial Thatcher, have been a great aid to our cause. Your plight has garnered more sympathy for humankind than anything we have tried in the last century. Not to mention the temptation you posed for Seizette, which put you in a perfect position to have the truth broadcast at exactly the moment it was most needed. I hope we can continue to count on your support in the difficult times ahead."

"Whoa," Spassel said. "He knows your name."

The Head Councilor smiled and asked, "And what's your name, young sir?"

"Oh! I'm Spassel Virtuewits. What an honor it is to actually meet you, Head Councilor. I would love to be Head Councilor one day. Have you ever considered taking on an apprentice?"

The Head Councilor chuckled and said, "I will now. A sprite is only as good as the company they keep, and it looks like you keep good company. I would love to have you and yours on my team."

Spassel looked to Nathanial with such ultimate joy he thought the little guy might explode.

"I need to get back to Mount Lassen and use that horrid device Seizette created to let the people know that I am back and ready to restore some semblance of peace," the Head Councilor said.

"Amaranth, will you join me? I'll need your help to operate that thing. Boss, can you get all of these brave sprites back to Sanctuary for recuperation? It will take some time to reopen the pro-factory plants and make sure the Swartza get the message to back off."

Amaranth and Boss both nodded and began to start accomplishing the cleanup.

"Aliya, is that you?" A girl's voice came from behind them. Aliya turned to see Jozy, coated in diamond dust. Her kind, round face was in a pout under the blue hair buns that were almost turned white from dust. Her grey-green eyes looked completely bewildered. "What's happening here?"

Aliya ran up and hugged Jozy. "Were you in the diamond?"

"I think so. I didn't want to attack a sprite who was asking for mercy in one of the trials. I think that disqualified me. How did I get here?"

"Seizette brought her prison along with her, and when she was destroyed, so was it. Everyone inside was freed," Aliya explained.

"Seizette was destroyed?" If it was possible, Jozy looked even more surprised.

"Come on, kiddos," Boss said to the group. "Help me do a headcount. Make sure all the students from Sanctuary are safe and together.

Gem, Bunny, and Phlegm, if you can start growing some wheels on those Swartza cages, we can send them along with the Head Councilor to Mount Lassen for judgment."

"Judgment?" Jozy asked. "I feel like I should point out that there are some Swartza who just did what they were ordered to because they were ordered to. They aren't all as bad as Seizette."

"I know. Don't worry," Boss said calmly. "We've been through a de-brainwashing epidemic before. Most of them will go to a facility that can explain to them the mental trauma they've endured. It has a high success rate of healing."

Jozy nodded and expelled a small sigh of relief. Aliya smiled encouragingly at her.

"Boss," Nathanial called. He was watching the Head Councilor and Amaranth gathering support from the Skilla to escort them back to the mountain on their birds. "Do you think the Head Councilor can stop the abuse that's happening on the humans first thing? They've caused a virus outbreak, and my mom has it."

Boss put a hand on Nathanial's shoulder. "You heard him. Re-opening the pro-factories is a top priority, which means first he'll be telling Big-Lyso to pull back on the outrageous 24/7 shifts their employees are operating on. I even have it on good authority that their CEO, Codfear Brack, is about to be unemployed. Everyone is going to be feeling a lot better in the morning. It's all going to be okay now, Nathanial. You did good." Boss stood up straight, then added, "Oh, and you can call me Conrad." A huge smile beamed across his face. Nathanial had never seen the like of such joy on that blue, brooding face before.

"Does that mean," Nathanial gaped, "your curse is broken?"

"That's right," Boss said proudly.

"That's amazing! You can finally be straight with me when I ask you a question." Nathanial pondered for a really good one to ask until he said, "Well, shoot. I think I already know everything there is to know about you."

Boss laughed a full-on belly laugh.

Nathanial crossed his arms, but the sight was contagious. He started laughing, too, when a memory struck him. "Wait, are you finding this so funny because of what you said to me that first day as my mentor… what was it? Something about the irony of you as my mentor. Well, yeah, it would have been nice to have had a *not cursed* mentor. Could have saved me a lot of snooping."

"Aw, Nathanial," Boss said, and did something else he had never done before: he hugged him.

"You really are stubborn."

"Hey!" Nathanial protested verbally but leaned into the hug with a smile.

"Now, let's get to work," Boss said, pulling back and looking around. "Lots to do before we sleep!"

Chapter 17

THE FINAL REBELLION

Everyone from Sanctuary wore their most colorful and elaborate celebration clothes for the beautiful afternoon out on the field. The topics sweeping through the crowd resonated with good news: Big-Lyso's monopoly was disassembled, lifting a great pressure off the sprite workforce and allowing Nathanial to breathe easy as human hospitals released recovered patients by the droves.

Family and friends had been invited to Sanctuary's event, and hundreds explored the fairground-like environment. Something resembling a Ferris wheel was in full buzz as shimmery green June bugs flew their giggling passengers around in circles. Youngsters floated a head or two above the crowds, sitting in dandelion seeds, while their parents trotted underneath holding a string, like their children were live kites. Merchants sold goods, most of them stamped with "I Survived the Fourth Rebellion," and shouted out their wares with gusto. A common design accompanying this declaration, was the outline of a sprite holding up a Truth Seer, the bold words glittering underneath.

Nathanial, Aliya, Mila, and Spassel walked along the booths with a couple of added friends. Mila had invited an old flame of hers, Zane—said flame seemingly rekindled as his black leather-clad arm was currently slung over her shoulder. He had to be a little older than her, as his colors were in full bloom. The dark purple around his eyes spread wide across the top of his face and continued back into the hair that stuck straight back on his head.

Spassel had invited Kadee, with whom he was very close from debate club at Hyperion. He was currently excitedly explaining to her the details of how Conrad Baldric, a figure from history he had portrayed many times in their club, was actually still alive and had been cursed into secrecy all these years.

"See, that's him over there," Spassel said, close to Kadee's ear, and pointed some seven booths away from them. Boss was putting a fine chain necklace with a little silver ship charm around Sarah's neck, and then gave the merchant some coin. Sarah kissed Boss on the cheek. "He's that blue color because of the curse, too. I asked him why he's still blue if the curse is broken, and he said it's because color doesn't make the sprite, it's their deeds. I didn't even know you could be a different blood class without changing your color. Neat, isn't it?"

Kadee looked completely enthralled as she hung on every word that came out of Spassel's mouth. Nathanial couldn't tell if she was budding her colors with those rosy cheeks or just blushing.

"Oh, look." Mila said, giving Nathanial a bump on the arm. "Skitzel. What do you say, Nat, should we have Aliya try some?"

"Oh, man." Nathanial burst out laughing. "I don't know."

Aliya curiously eyed the twisted food, which was knotted up in three different layers of powder-coated bread: green, orange, and yellow. "What's so special about it?"

"It's supposedly a training food for sprites. Like baby food, right, Mila?" Nathanial gave a crooked smile and remembered the mouth explosion he was teased for griping about at Hyperion.

"Oh, yeah," Mila agreed fervently. "Nathanial handled it just like a baby."

"Maybe later," Aliya decided after glances between the two goading her.

Jozy ran up from behind the group, her dimpled cheeks in full bloom with smiles. She was wearing an "I Survived the Fourth Rebellion" t-shirt and held up a fistful of bracelets printed with the same statement. "I got one for everybody!"

"Thanks, Jozy." Nathanial slipped it onto his wrist immediately. The bracelets she handed out were of many different colors; his was dark blue and rubbery, the words printed on it had shiny golden hues.

"Oh! Guess what I just heard?" Jozy said, hyped. "Swartza High is being closed for renovations. The diamond within the walls crumbled like the rest Seizette had grown and it destabilized the school. Not only that, but thanks to your notebook spreading through society like wildfire, Nat, parents are enraged to see what's been going on there. They've formed a new learning council that will take over teaching practices. They promise to end the lockdown and adopt learning techniques used at Hyperion."

"Wow!" Nathanial and the group delighted at the news with high fives.

They went for some nectar juice to celebrate, then came across Bunny and Gem at a ring toss game. An ice sprite operated the game, which gave an extra level of difficulty to any sprite aiming a frozen ring at the icicle spikes on the ground. Either the rings would stick to a sprite's hand as they tried to throw them quickly, or the rings would start to melt away if a sprite tried to aim for too long.

"Hey, guys," Bunny said to the group at large. "You got this, Gem."

Gem was on her last toss and hadn't managed to ring a spike yet. Her tongue stuck out the side of her mouth and she bounced on the spot. She threw her final ring and it swirled around an icicle tip until it landed firmly in place.

"Yes!" Gem jumped up, hands in the air, and turned to Bunny, who gave her a big hug.

"I knew you could do it!" Bunny shouted.

"Winner, winner, winner!" The ice sprite called out to the crowd and plopped a glowing hat on top of Gem's head that looked very much like an icicle.

The group clapped and laughed for Gem, who turned and took a bow.

"Well, it's about that time," Bunny said to everyone. "We'd better make our way to the very special reserved area that's awaiting us!"

Nathanial and his friends followed Bunny through the crowd toward the front, where a stage was set up. A few sprites gave Nathanial a pat on his back along the way. One even whispered, "I loved your notebook," into his ear.

Boss, Sarah, Ms. Colette, and Phlegm already stood in the patch of grass that was painted *reserved*. Nathanial recognized a teacher from

Hyperion on Phlegm's arm. It was Ms. Kaysea, a nectar sprite who taught nature tuning. She was the personification of honeysuckles: golden, sweet, and beautiful. Phlegm nodded at Nathanial as he arrived, smiling up at him. Aliya hugged her aunt before settling next to Nathanial in anticipation of the event.

Everyone's attention fell onto the Head Councilor, who was on stage and headed toward the podium.

"Good afternoon," he began, looking proud and strong. His antlered crown was a prong higher than usual, and his heavy tan robes were outlined with golden paisley trim. "This past week has perhaps been the most important week for us since the time leading up to the Crossing Treaty. Our foundation was rocked and the hope of a more tolerant and sustainable way of living was threatening to crumble. A call for new leadership had been demanded, with most sprites dolefully unaware of the false pretenses bolstering such.

"But, with a turn of luck, the very device that was created to manipulate and deceive the public against me ended up being exactly what we needed to bring honest facts into the light. With the public aware that voting for a new Head Councilor was tainted, we were able to turn back the vote to the question of whether or not new leadership was indeed needed at all.

"I've gathered you all here today to watch the results and see if our hard work has come to fruition as the voting results come in live across all sprite nations. Even if it is decided that I should no longer be Head Councilor, rest assured that does not mean my work for you will ever be finished. So long as I have the energy, I will fight for what is right."

The crowd applauded appreciatively as he stepped back and Amaranth brought the Truth Seer to the podium. She activated it and a tally board labeled *Head Councilor* appeared gargantuan above the stage. Far under the label were the choices of *Stay* or *Replace.*

There were moments of tense silence as the sprites in the crowd held their breath. Nathanial among them wondered what it would mean if the Head Councilor lost the vote and had to be replaced. This Head Councilor had been such an advocate for pro-factory living. Thanks to his quick action after Seizette's downfall, Codfear was no longer in charge of Big-Lyso, and his mother had recovered from her illness. Codfear was even to be prosecuted for gross manipulation of facts and aiding a conspiracy to undermine council law.

Nathanial was relieved to see Codfear joined by Malik and Cyron on that charge.

Still, Nathanial worried. These current hopeful events didn't mean the spite for humans had vanished altogether. If the Head Councilor was replaced with that wimpy looking Swartza pawn, Doctor Gustoes, for instance, Sprite society would continue their spiral down into the bleakness of human hate.

But then, like sand filling vials, the votes poured out in overwhelming favor of the Head Councilor. The crowd burst into a joyous roar.

Aliya hugged Nathanial so tight he thought he might faint from lack of oxygen.

Flowers exploded like fireworks overhead, sending gusting smells of lilac and lavender into the air.

Nathanial took the sweet scent deep into his lungs and gazed into Aliya's glossy, joyful brown eyes. The world behind her seemed to swim in a blur of color. Her freckles looked so cute over her nose and cheeks. Her lips were finally in that beautiful, hopeful smile he'd so long craved to see.

Nathanial leaned in and kissed Aliya. It was everything a first kiss should be: an accumulation of powerful sensations when anticipation and exhilaration collide. He was where he was meant to be, still and content, excited and alive.

Then, he was tackled. Mila, Spassel, Jozy, Bunny, and Gem circled Aliya and Nathanial in a ring-around-the-roses-style dancing hug.

It was with that carefree sentiment of celebration that the rest of the day and evening was spent. Sprites partook in all of the games, food, and fun with the confidence of increasingly better tomorrows.

Nathanial and Aliya were inseparable. There was hardly a moment when their hands were not clasped. They talked about all the places they would go and the things they could do. Nathanial explained all about how Hyperion worked and how much she was going to love going to school there.

Aliya told Nathanial about the Bridge of Ages, a huge construction built from human eyelashes that Mataunte had told her about when she was just a little girl. They decided it'd have to be the first place Bunny took them when they whisked their human families off into the sprite world.

With Aliya on his arm, it really did feel like all these things and more were just waiting for him. They sat and cuddled together under an "I Survived the Fourth Rebellion" blanket on the highest June bug of the Ferris wheel. They gazed out at the

Milky Way, which stretched out as countless stars above them in the clear night's sky.

This was the moment Nathanial had been wishing for, the moment adventure books had woven into his dreams during his everlasting isolation. He'd witnessed a flicker of good overcome overwhelming darkness and stood to roar with the oppressed.

As a last act of rebellion, from that night on, Nathanial determinedly lived a life that was happy, healthy, and free.

THE END

Words From The Author

I had completed the rough draft of *Nathanial Thatcher, The Fourth Rebellion* before the epic year of 2020 landed on us all. I gulped at the similarity of events that took place in my fictional world and in the real one, wondering if I had somehow set the sprites upon us. All our lives went topsy-turvy, watching helplessly as covid-19 rampaged around the world.

Finishing the book through the editing process while living a mirror of what Nathanial had went through, cooped up and unable to leave the house, gave me a greater connection to, and empathy for, his character. I feel that reflection comes through in the story. Though I always try to put fun and adventure in the mix, Nathanial's tale is full of the complex issues we discover during the trickery of growing up.

It's been a journey of my own just to complete and publish this series. When I started writing it, back in 2007, it was because I had been sick for months and no doctor could help with my cough. I decided to blame it on the sprites and I looked to Nathanial to help me find a way of beating them. I was struggling to find my own place in the world, working as a camera person in the film industry, wondering if I could find a way to write and direct one day. But it turned out I really preferred the writing style of books. Then the hurdle was how to publish? The road was still unclear. Finally, I stopped looking for the path most traveled and decided to make my own. My husband had a business degree, so why not start our own business? We founded Blue Dot Books and sent Nathanial out into the world.

Even if this story only ever finds itself a boutique audience, I am happy for each and every one of you. Thank you for traveling with me.